"I know that Venice needs help. I know that we must stop Expo." Small wisps of hair had come loose from Graziella's braid at the sides and they flew in different directions with the wind.

Percy had to work to take his attention away from how beautiful she was at that moment. "That's two points. But Domenico had four fingers up. What were the other two plans?"

Graziella looked away. "Similar things."

"What?"

"I cannot tell you now. I see the way you feel."

"People will get hurt?"

"Do not ask questions."

"Graziella, there has to be a better way."

She looked at him and said nothing.

"There has to be a simple, direct, effective way," said Percy.

Graziella squared her shoulders. "Then find it." She waited, and added much more softly, "Please."

Torcello
Burano

Murano

San Michele

VENICE

Mestre

Percy's
neighborhood

The Venetian
Lagoon

Adriatic Sea

Lido

0   25
miles

For the Love of Venice

Donna Jo Napoli

LAUREL-LEAF BOOKS

Published by
Dell Laurel-Leaf
an imprint of
Random House Children's Books
a division of Random House, Inc.
1540 Broadway
New York, New York 10036

Visit us on the Web! www.randomhouse.com/teens

Educators and librarians, for a variety of teaching tools, visit us at www.randomhouse.com/teachers

ISBN: 0-440-41411-3

RL: 6.1

Reprinted by arrangement with Delacorte Press

Printed in the United States of America

June 2000

10 9 8 7 6 5 4 3 2 1

OPM

Thanks to Susan Curcio, Wendy Lamb, Olivia Mo, Fiona Simpson, and Richard Tchen, all of whom wrestled details of Venice and plot and heart with me. Thanks also go to my family—for their usual role—especially to Barry and Nick.

working on the floodgate project consumed practically his every waking hour these days. The floodgate was a mechanical sea wall that would stop Venice from getting flooded when storms hit the Adriatic Sea. That's why they were spending the summer there—because of Dad's job.

The model stood only a foot high, but the actual floodgate was huge, he knew. And it was simple from a mechanical perspective: An electric motor made a massive wall of steel that was lying flat pivot upward until it was at a 60-degree angle. The sections of the floodgate would be placed side by side across the seabed of an inlet so that when they were raised, they would form a continuous steel wall, holding back the Adriatic waters from the lagoon. It was elegant in concept and design and Percy appreciated it the way he appreciated any well-designed machine. He was definitely his father's son when it came to anything mechanical. The floodgate would be a magnificent feat if it worked—and Percy wanted to see the actual floodgate. He wanted to very much. Just not this summer.

He pushed the map aside and sat down. This was the first time he'd sat at their dining room table in over a month. Dad's blueprints covered most of the table—and that huge waxy waterproof map with the garish colors covered the rest. The family had been forced to eat in the kitchen for all their meals. Dad didn't even seem to notice being squished together on the benches at the small kitchen table. Mom was so excited about finally going to

2

Venice that she'd eat standing up if it was better for Dad's project that way. She'd been to Venice when she was a college student, and she liked to say she'd been waiting ever since to return. She'd been taking intensive Italian lessons for the past year to get ready. And Christopher, who was only six, never seemed to know what was going on, and didn't much like food anyway.

Percy resented eating dinner in the kitchen, though. It was just one more way in which Dad's project wiped out the rights of all the rest of them. Or, at least, wiped out Percy's rights.

The phone rang.

Percy knew it was Vicky. He let it ring.

On the fifth ring, Percy heard Dad groan from the bedroom. Percy went into the kitchen and shut the door behind him, to block the noise. He sank down at the kitchen table.

On the twentieth ring Percy gave a rueful smile at Vicky's persistence, jumped up, and leapt for the phone on the kitchen wall. "Hello."

"I knew you were there."

"I knew you were calling."

"Listen, Percy, I asked my folks. They said you can live with us this summer. It's cool with them. Really."

Percy rubbed the sleep out of his eyes. He knew he'd made a mistake to tell Vicky his father wouldn't leave him behind to live alone all summer. That wasn't the main reason he was being forced to go to Venice. The main reason was Mom's conviction that Venice was an opportunity no one should be allowed to pass up. "That's really nice of them, Vicky. And of you, too. I appreciate it. I really do. But I've got no choice. The tickets are already bought."

"You can cancel a ticket."

"Not the kind Dad got—some supersaver thing. Look, it's not worth talking about."

"You're pooping out on me when you're supposed to be my racing partner, and it's not worth talking about?" Her voice rose. "We've been working for this summer for years! Finally—we're the best. Unbeatable!"

Percy almost smiled. Vicky was the only person he knew who could get away with using a kid word like *poop*. "I'm sorry. I wish I could stay as much as you do."

"My new boat's something else. My dad and I picked it up at Falmouth last night."

Percy imagined himself with Vicky, practicing all summer, then sailing in the big race in August. This summer they finally stood a serious chance of winning the junior cup. It was their last chance, too. Next summer he'd be a high-school graduate, so he'd be ineligible. He swallowed. "Torture me, why don't you?"

She gave a little laugh. "All right." Her voice was softer now. "Want to come over? I'll take you for a ride, as my passenger."

Percy nodded into the phone as if she could see him. "Sure. Let me get some clothes on. I'll be there in a half hour. See you."

"Yeah."

Percy hung up and pressed his forehead against the wall. He stood that way, leaning with his eyes closed, trying to steady his heartbeat. He wanted to sail—today and all summer long.

Mom came into the kitchen. "Vicky?"

"Mmmhmm." Percy stepped back from the wall and looked at his mother. She was short and slight, and he'd inherited her bone structure. When he was younger, he used to wish he'd been built on a larger scale, like Dad. He used to think he'd be better at athletics that way. But, in fact, his size didn't stand in his way in high school. He was quick and wiry and with enough practice, he was as good as the next guy. Often better.

He picked a tangerine out of the bowl on the kitchen table and watched Mom put coffee in the filter. He thought of starting the whole argument again, but he knew there was no point. She'd say he had the rest of his life for soccer and swimming and sailing and all his sports—she didn't distinguish among them. To her he was just her jock son. She couldn't understand how much this race meant to him—she refused to understand. She looked at him with her big vague eyes and nothing seemed to get through to her. It was maddening.

5

Mom lifted her chin as though she heard Percy's mental fight. "Transformation." Mom loved one-word sentences. "Just remember that, Percy—transformation."

Mom had been saying the light of Venice by day and the dark of Venice by night would startle them after living all their lives on Cape Cod. She was an artist and everything to her was the play of light, the shades and shadows of life. When Percy had tried to get her to explain exactly what she meant, she just smiled and said Venice would transform them, each of them, in unknown ways. That kind of airy talk was normal for Mom.

Percy peeled the fruit without a word and ate it, sweet section by sweet section.

He was going to Venice tomorrow no matter what. There was no way around it.

CHAPTER 2

Percy dropped his travel bag on the floor of the Marco Polo Airport with relief. The whole family drooped; they had traveled from the Cape to Boston to Milan to Venice, going the whole night and half a day without sleep.

Beyond the glass walls of the waiting area a string of wooden boats, lacquered to a bowling-alley shine, bobbed up and down in the lagoon. The late afternoon sun sparkled off the water. A sign on the dock by the boats invited, TAXI. Percy smiled: some words must be the same in all languages. That was comforting. "Hey, Dad," he said, his eyes on the boats.

Dad agreeably marched over to the taxis, asked the price, and gagged at the answer. Good old cheap Dad.

Percy laughed: Dad wasn't about to be transformed by Venice. That was a comfort, too.

They dragged their luggage on and off buses till they reached the parking area at the edge of Venice called the Piazzale Roma. They bought square slices of thick-crust pizza and trudged along the bank of a canal to their apartment—three flights up—feeling grimy and grouchy and otherworldly. Clothes somehow got stuffed into drawers and people somehow got tucked into beds.

When Percy woke later, it was pitch black. He looked at the glowing face of the alarm clock on his nightstand. Three A.M. Back home it was six hours earlier—nine o'clock on a Saturday night. His friends were going to movies and parties, having fun. And here he was, stuck in a place where he knew no one, didn't speak the language, and was doomed by his family's eccentricities. If he'd been home, he'd have been dancing right now.

No he wouldn't. Who was he kidding? If he'd actually gone to a party, he'd be standing on the sidelines wishing he could let himself go and just be a fool on the dance floor for once in his life. Wishing he was bold and interesting and had a girlfriend. But he probably wouldn't have gone. He probably would have spent the evening on some role-playing game—Magic, maybe—with his buddies Sam and Eric, and gone to bed at a reasonable hour and gotten up early to run before sailing with Vicky.

It wasn't a bad routine, actually. Sort of tame, but not bad.

And in the afternoons he would have worked as a lifeguard at the beach, like last summer. Their beach was a perfect place to swim and sail. The ocean was a perfect place to race.

Well, there was no point in thinking about home. Venice didn't look at all like Cape Cod. This was going to be a summer unlike anything he'd ever experienced.

He looked up through the dark at the ceiling that gradually took form as the sun rose. An ugly modern light fixture hung from the center of a plaster molding of grapes and pears. Evidence of a past whose luxury seemed otherwise totally gone. The desk against the wall was mahogany veneer, chipped at the edges. The bureaus were particleboard with a thin layer of white plastic on top, glossy and destructible, especially in the hands of someone like Christopher. Percy looked over at his little brother. Christopher slept soundly.

About the time Percy started to doze off again, he heard the familiar sounds of Dad organizing and rolling up blueprints. Percy got out of bed and sat on the couch in the living room. Mom was up, too. She kept running to the window to check the quality of the light as she packed a portfolio with papers, pencils, Cray-Pas. Percy watched listlessly. He yawned.

Mom gave quick, absentminded smiles. Suddenly she stopped and blinked, as if seeing him for the first time. "You better get dressed, Percy. And wake Christopher. It's almost eleven already. Dad wants to check in at the project, and you and Christopher and I have to find the perfect place to park our butts and draw."

"Christopher and I are supposed to hang around and watch as you draw?"

Mom's face dropped. "Of course not." But Percy could tell that Mom hadn't thought about how boring that would be for them. She was in her space cadet mode, as usual. She nodded now, half to herself. "You can go in and out of the churches nearby wherever I stop to work. You'll have fun. And we'll eat lunch in some nice little *osteria*. And . . ."

"You go by yourself, Mom. I'm too tired to move."

"What? Don't be silly. This is our first day in Venice. It's my dream come true. The problem is that you haven't eaten for so many hours. You have low blood sugar. That's it. You'll feel fine after breakfast." She looked around, grabbed her purse, and dashed out the door.

Percy looked to Dad for an explanation, but Dad had taken a blueprint back out of his briefcase and unrolled it. He leaned over it, tapping his fingers on the table edge, completely absorbed.

"Hey, Dad?"

"Hmm?"

Percy spoke louder: "Dad?"

Dad looked up at him with a question on his face.

"Don't you think Mom should go paint on her own today? I'll take care of Christopher. We'll wander around exploring. Okay?"

"Sounds like a good plan." Dad turned back to his blueprint.

Dad was so easy. As long as a request didn't cost money, Percy could rely on Dad's reasonableness. "Listen, when Mom comes back, be on my side, okay?"

"On your side?" Dad looked up with a touch of alarm on his face. "Did I miss something? Is this a fight?"

Mom came in just then with a dreamy look of satisfaction. She put coffee in Styrofoam cups, and thin grilled ham and cheese sandwiches on the table. "Toast," she announced.

Percy took a bite. "The name doesn't fit, but I admit these are decent."

"They're yummy." Mom smiled happily. "So, Percy . . ." She looked at him and her smile disappeared. "You're not dressed yet."

"I'm going back to bed."

"You can't spend all day in bed, jet lag or no jet lag. You'll never fall asleep tonight."

"I'll fall asleep. Look, when Christopher wakes up, we'll go exploring together."

"You're offering to take care of Christopher without being asked?"

Percy smiled. "It's a new me, Mom. Venice has transformed me."

Mom gave a doubtful smile. "But you want to go around Venice on your own?"

"He's gone in to Boston on his own," said Dad. "Boston's a lot bigger than Venice."

Percy shot Dad a thank-you with his eyes.

Mom looked from Percy to Dad. "They speak English in Boston."

"I've taken Spanish for years, Mom."

"Well, then," said Dad, clapping his hands together as though everything was settled. "Spanish, Italian, they're all the same."

Mom shook her head. "They're not all the same."

"I'm seventeen, Mom." Percy put his arm around his mother's shoulders. "I'll take good care of Christopher. And I'll give him a lot better time than he'd have tagging along after you."

"Here." Dad put a tourist map of Venice in Percy's hand. "And here." He gave Percy a wad of foreign bills. Percy couldn't believe his eyes. "That's about twenty dollars' worth. More than you'll need."

"The two of you planned this, didn't you?" Mom blinked several times.

Christopher stumbled into the room. He sank onto the couch.

Percy went over and sat by his brother. "Hey, Christopher, do you want to follow Mom around like a dog all day, or do you want to have fun with me?"

"I feel sick."

Not the best answer. But Percy could do something with it. "See? You can't drag him everywhere, Mom."

"Are you really sick, Christopher? Maybe we should all stay home." Mom came over and felt Christopher's forehead.

"He's just tired, Mom." Percy punched Christopher in the shoulder. "Aren't you, Christopher?"

"Can I have one of those sandwiches?" Christopher got up and took a toast.

"See?" said Percy. "He's fine. Go on, Mom. I'll take good care of him. We'll have a great time. You've been waiting for this day half your life. Go for it."

Dad touched Mom gently on the wrist. "There's time for everything, you know. Let's just ease into it. And for today, let's each do what we need to do."

Mom watched Christopher eat. "Well, I guess you're right. There's really no crime to speak of in Venice. And, Percy, you're good with a map. And, oh, all right. That's actually sort of nice for me." She stood taller as the realization hit her. "I can sit in one place all day if I want. I can absorb. That's what we all need to do today—look around. Absorb." She checked her pencils one more time. "Absorb," she sang to herself as she snapped the flap of her portfolio. She kissed Christopher on the cheek. "Is this really okay with you, honey?"

"Weird cheese. It sticks to my teeth." Christopher rubbed at his top teeth.

Percy had to admit it: Christopher always knew the right thing to say.

Mom came over and kissed Percy on the cheek. "Thank you, Percy." She slid a pack of charcoals into her pocket. "Thank you so much."

Then suddenly Mom and Dad were leaving, shooting instructions about the day—how to get hold of Dad in an emergency, where the landlord lived if anything went wrong, a dozen details about Venice they had already gone over before.

Dad handed Percy three keys: one to the downstairs gate, one to the building door, and one to their apartment. Then he clattered down the stairs.

Mom looked at the money that was still in Percy's hand. She added a handful of coins. Percy wanted to laugh—if all the bills Dad had given him added up to only twenty dollars, those coins probably weren't worth anything. But Mom looked proud of her addition. "Adventure," she said, as a pronouncement. And she was gone, too.

Percy stuck the money in his pocket. He was surprised

at how easy it had been to win Mom over. And he was a little tense about it, too. He rolled his shoulders backward and stretched his neck. What was he going to do all day?

Absorb.

Adventure.

CHAPTER 3

Sunlight made the boys squint as they walked along the Rio Nuovo. The opaque water lapped noisily whenever a boat passed. Percy held Christopher tight by the hand. Christopher had just learned how to swim, but who knew how deep these canals really were and what hid in the water?

They crossed a small bridge and walked down an alley with three-story buildings on both sides. The air was damp and dark. They turned at the end and walked through another alley and came out on an open area—which the map proclaimed to be a *campo*. The sun hit them again. But now, instead of sparkling off the water, it came like a wool blanket, heavy on their heads and shoulders. Even in his jet-lagged daze, Percy recognized that Mom was right: The light in Venice was different. When he was more awake, he'd have to pay attention. But for now he'd just wander.

Everything was dry in the *campo*s, dry and dusty. The walls seemed ancient—but, of course, they were ancient—with porcelain heads of angels and devils sticking out high up. Laundry swung on ropes that ran parallel to the sides of buildings right below the window levels on the second and third stories. People leaned out on their windowsills and talked to each other across the alleys.

They tramped from one *campo* to another, Christopher half-asleep and Percy alternately agog at the decorative pink facades of buildings and anxious at the unfamiliar sounds of Italian and the loud boat horns. Christopher's main objective, whenever he managed to keep his eyes open, was to find other six-year-olds to play with. But the only children they passed were preschoolers and toddlers with chattering mothers. Not a six-year-old in sight. Not a teenager in sight. All they managed to turn up was ice cream.

The ice cream store was close to their apartment—it was right in Campo Santa Margherita. When they passed it in the early afternoon, it was closed. But at five o'clock, when they were heading home, a woman was just opening it up.

"Ice cream, ice cream, you said you'd buy me ice cream if they opened up," shouted Christopher, suddenly finding the energy to be a pest.

"Shhh. You want everyone to know we're American?" Percy watched the light brown braid of the woman who was now setting up the green-and-white-striped cloth awning. Her braid swung as she went up on her toes to fasten the corners.

"What's wrong with being American?" said Christopher. "I want chocolate."

"Nothing's wrong with being American," whispered Percy. "Except that Venice is full of tourists and we're here for the summer; we're not tourists, so we might as well try not to act like them. It just makes people look at us." Her braid was really a braided ponytail, high up and bouncy. She wore a white skirt and blouse—maybe that was what all Italian ice cream vendors wore? Her calves were deeply tanned and well developed. The legs of a soccer player. Percy stopped and flexed his toes upward. He felt his own big calves tighten. Mom said all Italians played soccer, but he didn't believe her. She'd spewed sweeping generalizations all winter when she was talking up this trip.

"You're being self-conscious," said Christopher, "just like Mom says. And look, they've got the good kind of cone, not that soggy kind we got in the airport."

"Can't you whisper?" whispered Percy.

"I'm little," said Christopher. "You can't expect me to do everything right."

"If you're old enough to use a word like *self-conscious,* you're old enough to whisper when I ask you to."

The woman went inside and banged things around under the refrigerated counter. The ice cream sat on top of the counter in rectangular containers behind glass.

"And I don't have to do everything you tell me to just because you're older," said Christopher loudly.

"That's right. You have to do everything I tell you to because if you don't, I'll pulverize you."

"Oh," said Christopher in a whisper. He took Percy's hand and looked up into his face with frightened eyes.

"It's okay," whispered Percy. "I won't hurt you, dork brain. Just let's go quietly into the store and I'll order your ice cream for you and you won't say a word, okay?"

Christopher nodded earnestly.

Percy read the sign: 1500 LIRE. He reached into his jeans pocket and counted out the exact amount. He could do it. Easy. Just walk in. Say, *"Cioccolato."* Walk out. He'd had five years of Spanish between high school and junior high already and Spanish and Italian were a lot alike; how hard could it be to pull off being Italian if he said only a single word?

Percy waited for Christopher to lead the way into the store. But Christopher stood rigid, clutching his hand.

Percy wished he hadn't said he'd pulverize him. Percy stepped forward at precisely the same moment that Christopher decided to step forward. They squeezed through the doorway together and Percy stepped on Christopher's foot.

"Ow," said Christopher loudly. "I mean, ow," he whispered.

"Sorry," whispered Percy.

The woman stood up from behind the counter. Only she was a girl, with rich olive skin and luminescent black eyes and a wide mouth that now curved into a smile, revealing deep dimples in her cheeks. Percy studied her angular jaw, her thin long nose that began immediately below those high eyebrows. The little wisps of hair at her temples had red highlights and she wore gold hoop earrings that sparkled like her white white teeth in that smile. Everything brought Percy back to her beautiful smile, which now moved with the words, *"Buona sera. Vorreste?"*

It wasn't polite to stare. Percy forced a smile. How old could this marvelous girl be? And how could he answer her without coming across as a dunce? *Buona sera* he knew: good afternoon or evening. The rest must mean something like "Come on and order." Okay. That's what he came in for. Right. Yeah. Okay. And he had better hurry; she was looking at him as though suspended in time, but that couldn't last much longer. He cleared his throat. *"Cioccolato."* Not too bad.

She held her hand with the scooper over the chocolate. *"Un cono o una coppetta?"* Her eyes moved quickly to the cone dispenser and the stacks of little paper cups.

That was an easy one. *"Cono."*

She smiled and pulled a cone from the dispenser.

Christopher put both hands on the glass case and watched with his mouth open. The girl laughed. She filled the cone expertly with a few swift moves and held it out to Christopher. *"Per te?"*

Christopher accepted it with a grin and took a big greedy bite.

Percy leaned down and whispered in Christopher's ear, "Say *grazie.*"

"But you told me not to talk," said Christopher loudly.

"Americani?" asked the girl.

"Yeah," mumbled Percy. *"Sì."*

The girl smiled and looked at Percy expectantly. Her eyes seemed to laugh at him. He felt rooted to the spot. Maybe he should reach out and shake hands and say *piacere,* which meant "pleasure." Mom had told Percy that Italians always told each other what a pleasure it was to have met. No word would have been more sincere right now. Percy took a deep breath to prepare to speak that one, most important word. The girl watched him with amusement.

"Pay her," said Christopher at last.

The girl laughed.

Percy flushed and put the money on the counter. *"Grazie."*

The girl looked surprised. *"E per te? Niente?"*

Percy shook his head in confusion.

The girl pursed her lips. Then she pointed at each flavor, one after the other. *"Questo? O questo?"* She invited him with a smile. It was one of those offers you couldn't refuse.

Percy looked at the sign over the chocolate chip. *"Stracciatella."*

"Stracciatella," she said slowly, exaggerating the *l*'s. *"Stracciatella."* The way she said it, it was the most wonderful word he'd ever heard.

"Stracciatella," said Percy.

"Bravo." She gave a quick nod and dipped the scooper into water to clean it off. A man came into the store with two small boys. The bigger boy stuck his tongue out at Christopher. Christopher moved closer to Percy and dripped chocolate onto Percy's white sneakers. *"Buona sera,"* said the ice cream girl to the man and the boys. *"Un momento solo."* She filled a cone with peach ice cream and held it out to Percy.

Percy opened his mouth to object, but he didn't know the Italian words. Hadn't she understood him when he'd said *stracciatella?* Hadn't she said *bravo* to praise him? He stood silent with his mouth open.

The girl laughed.

The smaller of the two little boys stood on tiptoe and licked the glass of the ice cream case.

The man grumbled. The bigger boy pulled the little one backward and the little one turned and bit the bigger boy on the chin. The man put a hand on each boy's head and spoke firmly.

The ice cream girl still held the cone in front of Percy's face.

The peach ice cream did look good. Percy took it and pulled Christopher by the hand out the door.

It was only a five-minute walk back to the apartment, but in those five minutes Percy finally woke up fully. He saw the early evening light glisten on the water. He heard the strange call, *"Ooooeeee, ooooeeee, ooooeee,"* as a gondola rounded the corner of his canal. Even though Dad had told him the *gondolieri* called out warnings to other boats as they turned corners, hearing that cry out of the blue still sent shivers down his spine. He looked around at all the oleanders, Mom's favorite flowers, peeking out over tall walls, gently scenting the wet air. The sight, the sound, the smell, the feel of everything were new and fresh and wonderful. He was, indeed, in Venice. This wasn't just Marco Polo's birthplace; it was the famous city of romance, as Mom said. The jewel of Italy. Maybe, just maybe, she wasn't all wrong and there was something worth doing here after all.

CHAPTER 4

Mom and Dad were dressed and ready to go when Percy and Christopher came in the door. "Ice cream," said Mom with a little *tsk* as she wiped chocolate from Christopher's chin. "You know we're going out to dinner."

"Think of the calcium," said Percy.

"Thanks." Mom's voice was flat. She twirled her earrings with both hands and looked through Percy, preoccupied. He was used to that kind of look; it was Mom's habit. Mom smiled suddenly at some private delight. "Get dressed. I want to take you the long way there, stopping in a couple of churches. And we have to buy flowers."

Dad looked surprised. "Flowers?"

"People here bring flowers when they're invited to someone's house for dinner. A woman I met at the french fry *osteria* told me."

"What's the french fry *osteria*?" said Christopher.

"A nice place for lunch that's famous for its french fries. I'll take you there."

As they walked to the woman's house (Marina somebody, another civil engineer), the crowds got thicker and thicker. Percy was amazed. In their small excursion today through the area right around their apartment, Percy and Christopher had passed mostly locals going about their daily business. But this Marina lived across town and to get there they were obviously passing by the most popular haunts. Sometimes it was so crowded, people jostled each other. More than once, Percy reached for Christopher's hand. He didn't trust the crowds not to knock his brother into a canal.

They arrived at Marina's house at seven—right on time, because Mom had woven a mad path around clumps of tourists bent over maps, and Dad and Percy and Christopher had followed like obedient ducklings. But Marina didn't serve dinner till well past eight. Christopher would have been starving if it hadn't been for the ice cream Percy had bought him. When Dad and Marina pulled out blueprints and started talking about the floodgates, Mom sat on the couch next to Percy and whispered, "I'm sorry I got mad about the ice cream. You probably saved Christopher's life."

Percy smiled magnanimously. He felt grown up and responsible.

Dinner was elegant—a giant whole fish grilled with no spices or condiments at all. It was delicious. The *tortellini* that came first were tender. The salad was unusual—zingy. The lettuce itself had a sharp taste. And the cheese tray that followed was smelly but wonderful. When the huge crystal bowl filled to the brim with balls of all different-flavored ice cream was set in the middle of the table, Percy thought he would burst. Instead, he fell into a gentle reverie about ice cream—and then a gentler one about ice cream vendors.

On the way home, they walked through tiny alleys that were mercifully free of tourists. Percy stretched his arms out and touched the walls on both sides. Christopher broke away from Dad's hand and fell back beside Percy. He leaned sleepily against Percy's arm and whispered, "Why do Italian women have three vaginas?"

"What!" Percy jumped away from Christopher and slammed his shoulder against the wall. He looked down at Christopher's face. In the dark he couldn't see his brother's expression, but he knew from his voice that Christopher was completely serious. "What gave you that idea?"

"I saw them."

"You saw them!" Percy almost shouted.

"Well, I saw two of them. On two women."

"What women?" said Percy, his voice rising. He took Christopher by the hand and pulled him close as if for safety.

"The ice cream lady and that lady Marina we just ate with."

Percy's ice cream girl? He slowed down now, to let Mom and Dad get farther ahead so there was no chance they could hear any of this. "What are you talking about?" Percy felt weak. He leaned over his brother and whispered, "Did you look under the ice cream girl's dress?"

"I wouldn't do that. Don't you know anything?"

Percy straightened up. "So where did you see them?"

"Under her arms."

Percy burst out laughing.

Dad and Mom stopped. "What's so funny?" called back Dad.

"Those are armpit hairs," Percy whispered to Christopher. "Lots of women shave their armpits. But if they didn't, everyone would have hair there. Women are just like men in that way." Percy took Christopher by the hand and caught up with their parents.

"What was it?" said Dad.

"Just something between us guys." Then Percy said to his mother in a mysterious tone, "You sure did a lousy job on sex education for this one."

"Huh?" said Mom.

Within twenty minutes Percy lay in bed thinking of hairy places and ice cream. That was when he realized he hadn't paid for his peach cone. Oh no. The girl must think he was a real jerk.

In the morning Percy went with Mom to the bakery in Campo Santa Margherita. Percy looked across the wide *campo*. The ice cream store was closed, of course. But the bakery had obviously been open for hours. Most of the bread from the first buying spree was gone, but there was still plenty to choose from. The bakery woman went on and on to Mom. The words for *hour* and *bread* stuck out—almost exactly like the Spanish. Percy knew the woman was reassuring Mom that within an hour, the bins would be full again. Mom smiled and chattered back. Then she bought thick, flat bread, covered with salt, oil, and small black olives. *Focaccia*. It smelled as good as anything Percy had ever smelled before. They stopped at the *latteria* for milk and cheese and juice, then headed home.

When they got back, Dad had already made coffee and was urging Christopher along in getting dressed.

"What's the hurry?" said Percy. He had already planned his day with Christopher. They would take the boat from the Ca' Foscari stop nearby and go to Piazza San Marco— the most famous square of Venice, where the great palace was. From there they'd wander back to the Campo Santa Margherita, where they'd buy two double-scoop ice cream cones.

"We're going to Cannaregio," said Mom happily. "It's a good twenty-minute walk."

"Cannaregio?"

"Venice is divided into six areas, called *sestieri*. Our apartment is in Dorsoduro, and the next *sestiere* over is Cannaregio." She poured a cup of coffee and leaned back against the counter. "Where'd you find this coffee, Vince?"

"Back of the cupboard," called Dad from the bedroom.

"Stale. But it'll do for today."

"Mom," said Percy, "do you think we could finish a conversation for once?" He poured himself coffee.

Mom focused on Percy with what looked like difficulty. "You know, you've been developing a sense of patience since you turned seventeen, but it still has a way to go. You remind me of my father. I wonder if it wasn't a mistake to name you after him."

Percy repeated the word *patience* to himself. Then he felt a twinge of remorse. Mom couldn't help it if she drifted like this. It was probably part of what made her an artist. And he was proud that she was an artist. He was proud that she seemed to have so little use for money and that she focused on the odd small beauties of life. She was out of her element in the ordinary world—vulnerable. A stab of protectiveness for her overcame him. "What's in Cannaregio, Mom?" he asked gently.

Dad and Christopher sat at the table. Mom poured Dad coffee and Christopher milk.

Christopher took a gulp. "Yuck. The cow must be sick."

Mom sank into a chair. "Milk tastes different in every country. You'll get used to it."

"Mom," said Percy, moving so that he stood close beside her. "Mom, what's in Cannaregio?"

"A day camp run by the Salesiani priests. If it works out, Christopher will be busy all day."

Percy choked on his coffee. "A church camp for Christopher? Christopher doesn't know the first thing about Catholicism. Or about Christianity, for that matter. He doesn't even know what a prayer is. He's going to hate this camp."

"Don't say that." Mom's face went red.

Dad gave Percy a shut-up-now stare.

Christopher looked at Percy with wide eyes.

"Hey, what's going on? Don't spaz over it." Percy looked from Dad to Mom. "You're the ones who raised us atheists."

Mom took a slice of *focaccia*. "He'll love Don Bosco." She nodded. "You will, won't you, Christopher?"

Christopher looked down into his milk. "There's things floating around in here."

"Who's Don Bosco?" asked Percy.

"He's a saint now," said Mom, "but he was a man who loved children and did all sorts of things for them."

"Things?" said Percy.

"Don't ask me." Mom took an olive pit out of her mouth and set it on her plate. "You know I don't know that junk."

"That's my point," said Percy.

"No, you don't have a point," said Dad, reaching for a slice of the *focaccia*. "My parents met at a dance at Don Bosco."

"In Venice?" said Percy in amazement.

"God, this is good." Dad held his *focaccia* up and looked at it from several angles. "Have a piece, Percy."

Percy sighed. Now Dad was doing it, too. It was contagious. "Did your parents meet in Venice?" he asked slowly.

"Brookline, Massachusetts. There are Don Bosco churches all over the world. And all of them have the mission of doing good for young people."

"But Grandpa doesn't even go to church," said Percy.

"He doesn't anymore," said Dad.

"Maybe because he met Grandma there," mumbled Percy.

"What?" said Dad.

"Nothing."

"Can I have some of that bread?" asked Christopher.

"Focaccia." Mom pushed the plate toward Christopher. "And, come to think of it, I was doing volunteer work at Don Bosco when I met your father."

"Oh, yeah." Dad got a mushy look on his face. "I'd forgotten about that."

"You forgot how we met?" said Mom.

"You did, too, for a minute at least." Dad took another bite of *focaccia* and spoke with his mouth full. "But I remember now. Oh, yeah. Mmmhmm."

"Don Bosco," said Mom pensively.

"Hey, folks, are you still here?" Percy put down his coffee cup and waved his arms in front of their faces. "So if you love this Don Bosco so much, why didn't you raise us Catholic?"

"Don't act foolish, Percy," said Dad, snapping out of his sappy spell.

"To be Catholic, you have to believe. To appreciate Don Bosco, all you have to do is watch what goes on." Mom smiled at Percy. "Our landlady sent me information about this camp, but I didn't say anything earlier because I wanted to ask around a bit. Last night at dinner I heard good things about it." She looked happily at Christopher. "Christopher is going to love Don Bosco." Then she smiled at Percy. "Then you can have your adventure. Or adventures. I assume you don't want to spend your days with me, after what you said yesterday."

"You assume right." But Percy's stomach still fluttered. He ate his breakfast in silence. What if by some miracle Christopher actually liked the day camp? What would Percy do alone all day? He'd have to try to meet people. People his own age. People whose language he didn't speak. But he hadn't seen a single person his age yesterday, when he and Christopher had gone walking. Some adventure.

Maybe he hadn't seen them because he'd been too tired to notice. Was that possible?

And, oh yes, he had seen one, one very important one: the ice cream girl.

Probably all the people Percy's age worked all summer, the way the ice cream girl did.

As soon as Mom and Christopher left the apartment, Percy made his way back to Campo Santa Margherita, armed with 1500 lire and the apology he'd dug out of the Italian phrase book: *Mi dispiace*. But the store was still closed. Not much demand for ice cream at ten minutes after nine in the morning. He decided to explore until the ice cream store opened.

The buildings here and everywhere else he'd been so far in Venice formed one continuous wall. Percy stopped and scrutinized the wall. Someone had spray-painted EXPO NO! in giant black letters across the center and there were old announcements of art exhibits, most of them faded and tearing at the edges. Stucco had fallen off in big patches, showing the bricks underneath. Why did Italians like to live in neighborhoods that looked like bombed-out slums? Last night they had gone through a shambles of an alley and then come upon a beautifully varnished door. The door had opened and they'd stepped inside onto a marble floor with twelve-foot ceilings and plaster moldings all around of naked babies with wings carrying baskets of fruits and flowers. Marina's home was a palace. Behind any one of these unassuming walls there might be another palace. And the people who lived in them might be royalty—at least they would have been, if Italy hadn't united and become a republic. Real royalty.

With a real princess.

Dressed all in white.

Very un-American. Undemocratic. Un-twentieth-century. Unreal.

Dad said refusing to come to terms with the passing of time had put Venice in trouble today. A city in decay. Dad was here to try to fix that—to bring modern technology to the water control problem. What would the people who lived in these houses have said if they'd known that a lot of people outside Venice thought it was time for the city to change? Change or die, that was what Dad said.

So much of Venice was hidden from the tourist's eye. After last night's crowd, Percy understood why—that was the only way the Venetians could survive the influx of tourists. Percy stepped backward to take a long look at the wall and speculate about the lives that went on behind it. He bumped into a young man in a suit. "Uh . . ." What was that word? *"Scusi, signore."*

"Prego," the man shot out over his shoulder, not missing a step. He crossed the nearest bridge and disappeared. Venetians moved quickly. Probably anybody who looked out a window could tell he wasn't Venetian just by the fact that he was meandering.

He kicked an apple core. It rolled through a squashed dog turd and fell into the canal with a soft splash. Percy had been dodging dog turds all morning. People should curb their dogs. Except there weren't grassy strips along the walks in Venice. There were only stones right up to the canals, what Mom had told him were called *fondamenta*. But surely they could set aside areas—maybe a park that was nothing but a dog toilet.

Come to think of it, Percy hadn't seen a single park yet. There were lots of private gardens. Trees stuck up behind walls, like the one across Rio Nuovo with the oleander. The tops of the walls had large jagged spikes of glass stuck into cement. Sometimes a foot-high ring of rusty barbed wire. Italians certainly knew how to get their message across. And so Percy was bound to spend the summer without any open space to kick a ball in. Okay, so he'd only arrived Saturday night and now it was just Monday morning. What did he really know about Venice? Nothing.

And so what if it didn't have parks? It had all this water. Almost everywhere he walked, there was water beside him—water you couldn't drink and shouldn't swim in, but still water. Sometimes there were steps down that just kept going under the water, like an invitation to an undersea kingdom. Percy felt a sudden itch to swim. He had to try to get out to Venice's beach, the Lido, soon. And maybe he could find a sailing club somewhere. That was an idea. Maybe they'd let him join for the summer.

He came to a corner, turned left, and suddenly found himself with a soccer ball rolling right at him, as though challenging his very thoughts. He kicked it automatically toward the group of kids, who looked like they were about ten or eleven.

"Grazie," said a boy. He dribbled away with the ball.

This place was unusual: a long wide rectangle with trees set into plots of dirt about five feet square. It wasn't surrounded by shops—so it wasn't a *campo.* It was just a big avenue with a small fountain in the center. Percy's step quickened. He could buy a cheap soccer ball and come here in the middle of the afternoon, when everyone was eating the traditional midday meal Mom talked about. He'd have the place to himself.

The noise of TVs came from the big orange and yellow buildings. It gave a kind of lazy, hazy sense to the day.

Percy liked it. He walked near one wall and stayed out of the way of the ballplayers.

The wall gave way to a waist-high railing. About four feet beyond the rail running parallel to it was a brick wall, at least twenty feet high. And behind the brick wall were three tall stuccoed buildings with small, barred windows. The brick wall was thick enough to have a walk on top, interrupted by turrets at the corners. Two stone lion heads with rings in their mouths were mounted on the wall. The whole effect made Percy think of a castle. He half expected someone to fire guns from the walk, like in a battle in another century. The only thing out of place was a soccer ball stuck on the edge of one roof, held in place by a broken tile, probably doomed to stay there forever.

A man appeared on the wall, dressed in a sky-blue uniform with a beret that had a large medal on it. Percy couldn't believe his eyes: The man carried a rifle. No, not a rifle, a submachine gun. He walked the length of the brick wall. At the far corner he stopped and another man in uniform joined him. They talked. Then they passed each other.

Percy felt his heart speed up. Automatic weapons in the middle of a residential neighborhood? Children played ball not more than forty feet away. He ran his hands along the railing, which was already warm from the morning sun. A few feet down there was a sign on the wall. His Spanish helped—it said to stay at least two meters away. And now

Percy could see words chiseled into the side of the middle of the three buildings. *Prigione* was the only one that mattered. It was a prison.

Percy stepped back from the railing and walked parallel to it all the way to the end. He didn't see anyone looking out from those windows. The wide avenue ended in a canal. But there was a sidewalk that led behind the prison, between the prison rail and the canal. Percy turned onto the sidewalk. He looked up again. The guard on top watched him. Percy thought of the peach ice cream cone he hadn't paid for. He laughed. The guard kept watching him.

At the middle of this side of the building was the official entrance to the prison. Opposite was a bridge that crossed the canal. But unlike any other bridge Percy had seen in Venice, this one had a tall gate on the end closest to the prison.

The electric gate was opening just at that moment. A cluster of women walked across the bridge with their backs to him. They passed over onto the other *fondamenta* and one of them pressed a button on a pole. Percy watched the gate move slowly till it clanged shut behind them.

The group broke up and Percy saw a light brown braid swing as a girl in blue-and-white-striped pants ran down an alley and was lost to sight. The stripes of the girl's pants weren't prison garb, Percy felt sure of that, but they seemed menacingly appropriate.

Percy ran to the bridge and shook the gate. There was no way to open it without the key that fit into the box that controlled the electric opener. A tingle crept up Percy's spine. Everything seemed fine on the surface, but he had the sensation that nothing truly was. A prison sat in the middle of a sleepy neighborhood. A girl with a braid had crossed to the other side of a locked gate. Venice might not be what it appeared to be at all.

CHAPTER 5

"Want an ice cream, Christopher?" Percy swung his legs over the edge of the couch and sat up. He closed the issue of his cycling magazine and set it on the coffee table beside Mom's newest sketchpad. "How about it? Let's go."

Christopher didn't look up from the battle scene he had spread out on the floor. "You took me for ice cream last night and the night before and the night before that. I'm sick of it." He rolled a green plastic tank straight into a man on horseback. The man went down with a scream: "Ahhh!"

"Oh, come on, Chris, you love chocolate ice cream." Percy walked over to his brother and squatted beside him. "Come on."

Christopher's tank rolled on relentlessly, plowing down another man on horseback. "Ahhh!"

Percy went to the shelf and brought back an airplane. He flew it over the tank. *"Bababaa-a-a-a-a!"* He knocked the tank over with a flick of his finger. "Your tank's dead. Let's go get ice cream."

"He's not dead, he's just wounded." Christopher righted the tank. "Anyway, we got ice cream at Estate Ragazzi today."

"The priests give you ice cream?"

"Not the priests, the *animatori*—the teenagers who teach us all the activities." Christopher's tank rolled on toward the next group of men on horses. "The priests hardly do anything except yell at the end of the day about all the bad things we did."

"How do you know they're yelling about all the bad things you did?" said Percy.

"Huh? 'Cause they are," said Christopher.

"I mean, how can you understand what it's about? It's in Italian."

"I know some Italian: *Buon giorno, ciao, aspetta.*"

"What's that mean, *aspetta*?" said Percy.

" 'Wait.' That's what I say to them all the time: *Aspettami*. Because they're always going too fast." The tank killed another four men and horses.

Percy screwed up his mouth. Here was dumb little

41

Christopher getting the chance to learn Italian the natural way every day, while Percy, who really liked learning languages, stayed home alone and tried to learn it from a dictionary and his stupid little phrase book.

Oh, he did other things, too. When Christopher got home from camp each afternoon, Mom took them to a tourist sight. So far they'd seen the Doges' Palace, the Rialto Bridge, and some church with a long name. The palace was the best, especially the huge conference room with the biggest ceiling in the world that has no visible vertical supports other than at the edges. He loved climbing up into the attic and looking from above at how it was built. And he shivered when they passed the prison cells off a central room where centuries ago you could hear the screams of people being tortured. So many things in Venice seemed mixed that way—something stupendously wonderful with something stupendously awful.

And during the morning and early afternoon, when Percy was alone, he did a little wandering on his own—mainly past the ice cream store. About six or seven times a day. But the girl with the braid was never there. He'd seen her last on Sunday afternoon with Christopher. And then maybe on Monday morning, on the bridge behind the prison. But maybe that hadn't even been her. After all, he hadn't seen the face of the girl on the bridge.

Now it was Wednesday night and Percy had already finished the three novels he'd brought with him for the summer and his regime of working out in his bedroom with the push-up bars an hour a day and practicing soccer with his new ball in the wide avenue by the prison for another hour had already become tedious. He needed friends. Or at least some excitement. He needed to find out about a sailing club—but for that he'd have to ask Mom for help and he resisted that idea. He sort of liked having his own life here—a life no one else knew anything about. "Listen, Christopher, if you come to the ice cream store with me, I'll buy you a cone with whipped cream on top."

"I like whipped cream," said Christopher.

"I know."

Christopher went to the hall closet. He put on his shoes. "Let's go."

Percy eyed Christopher's shoes. They were made of green cloth and the bottoms were rubber. "I like your new shoes."

"Marcialunghe," said Christopher.

"What?"

"That's what they're called. All the kids wear them."

"All the little kids," said Percy.

"No, even the kids your age. The *animatori* at the program wear them."

"Does *animatori* mean 'counselors'?"

"I don't know," said Christopher. "That's just what we call them. They're washable."

Percy put his face down near Christopher's. "The *animatori* are washable?"

"Give me a break." Christopher made a crazy face, opened the door, and raced down the stairs.

Percy followed. The evening air was cool and dry. They walked to Campo Santa Margherita and Christopher got his *cioccolato,* this time with *panna montata,* whipped cream. Percy read the words easily off the sign and it seemed true what his mother said: You could pronounce Italian pretty much correctly just by looking at the spelling. Or maybe it was just that no one bothered to correct him. He paid the ice cream woman, the same one who had been there since Monday, the one who had no braid and no dimples and wore an ordinary flowered sundress. He didn't even have to go into the ice cream store, because the woman served him from the counter that opened right onto the *campo.* Percy felt cheated.

In fact, it wasn't just the ice cream store. He looked around at all the walls. This whole city seemed to shut him out. Nothing to do. No friends. No language, even.

Christopher ran to a vacant bench in the center of the *campo.* There were two other kids over by the fountain. Both had on *marcialunghe* shoes. Christopher could have been Italian, sitting there so carefree on the bench, swinging his *marcialunghe,* licking busily. But Percy still looked totally American. He sat down heavily beside Christopher.

"Why don't you ever get a cone?" asked Christopher.

"I'm waiting," said Percy.

"For what?"

"Not what, who."

"For who?" said Christopher.

Percy frowned. "Not who, whom."

"Make up your mind," said Christopher. "Whom what?"

Percy scratched his head. "The girl with the braid."

"What girl with the braid?" said Christopher.

"The one who gave us ice cream the first time we came here. You probably didn't notice her . . ."

"Oh, Graziella," said Christopher. He slurped his dripping cone.

"What did you say?"

"Graziella." Christopher held his cone up and bit off the bottom. He sucked at it. "That's her name."

Percy stood and faced Christopher. "How do you know her name?"

Christopher sucked the rest of the ice cream out through the bottom. "She's one of the *animatori*."

"You're kidding."

Christopher munched his cone and ran to the fountain. He washed his hands. "She teaches *filografia*."

Percy followed him. "What's that?"

"We bang nails into a board, then we run a string from nail to nail."

Percy furrowed his brows. "What for?"

"We make designs. Graziella likes mine. She said it's *bello*."

"Maybe it isn't the same girl."

"Yes it is."

"Lots of girls have braids," said Percy.

Christopher ran ahead, then stopped in front of a store window.

Percy followed, muttering to himself, "Lots of girls wear hoop earrings. Lots of girls have wide eyebrows." He caught up to Christopher.

Christopher pointed. "Buy me that deck of cards. Please, Percy. You've got enough money."

Percy looked at the box. Four cards were fanned out across the front, with mysterious figures on them. "How do you play with them?"

"I don't know. But everyone has them. There are stories for each of the pictures."

"What kind of stories?"

"I can't understand enough Italian yet to know. I need them, Percy. Please."

Percy looked at the sign, then counted his money. He went in and bought the deck. Christopher waited outside, his eyes anxious. When Percy handed him the deck, his smile was huge.

"Thank you."

Percy laughed. How easy it was to make Christopher happy. His mind could bop around from one thing to another, fast and free, while Percy went round and round with the same thoughts for hours.

Christopher ran down the alley, over the bridge, and along the canal. He rang the buzzer at their apartment building.

Someone hit the lock release from inside the apartment and the gate to the front garden swung open.

Christopher looked back at Percy. "Her *marcialunghe* are black." He ran ahead into the building.

Percy closed the gate behind them, half-upset that even Christopher realized he was still thinking about the ice cream girl. He walked the fifteen feet through their excuse for a garden. In the midst of brown grass one lonely rosebush did its best to cover a huge trellis that had seen better days. This apartment didn't have a loving occupant anymore—instead, students lived in it all through the year and if Percy's family hadn't taken it now, it would have sat empty for the summer. At the very top of the rosebush, three little buds reached for the sun. Percy wondered what color they would be. Red would look good beside a light brown braid. Pink would, too. Yellow? Sure. Any color. Percy thought about black *marcialunghe* on the ice cream girl's tanned feet.

He ran up the stairs and burst into the apartment. "Mom, Dad, I have to find something to do with my time."

Mom and Dad sat at the dining room table before a

spread-out map. "Funny you should say that, Percy. I was just talking to your mom about you coming with me to the CNR tomorrow." Dad smiled and pointed to the map. "Take a look at this."

"Come with you?" Percy's tone said it all: This was not what he had in mind.

Dad's smile faded. His finger pointed at the map insistently and a tightness crept into the corners of his eyes. He turned his attention to the map, but his stiff shoulders showed that he was waiting for Percy to speak.

Percy recognized the situation—Dad hated to have his plans undone, especially when he'd thought his offer would be such a treat. And that offer would have been a treat normally—it would have been a more wonderful opportunity than Percy would ever have expected. This wasn't a normal time, though. Percy looked to Mom for help.

Mom looked baffled. "You love helping Dad on projects at home, Percy. What's the matter?"

Percy couldn't tell them about the ice cream girl; that would make him look like an idiot. After all, he'd spoken all of six words to her. He silently mouthed the words to his mother so that his father wouldn't know what he'd said: I don't want to work with Dad now.

Mom looked down at her hands. She hated confrontations.

Percy faced his father uncomfortably. "So what is this CNR?"

"Centro Nazionale delle Ricerche, the national research center. The people I've been writing to all year about the design of MOSE work there." MOSE was the name of the floodgate project—it was an acronym for something, but Dad said it was particularly appropriate because it made people think of Moses parting the waters.

"That woman Marina," said Percy.

"Exactly. Marina and Paolo and a whole team. We've already got that project well under way, of course, with the prototype set up at Porto di Malamocco. Everything's ahead of schedule, even." Dad tapped the map at the spot between the two southernmost islands in a string that made up the blockade between the Adriatic Sea and the lagoon. "But there are a number of other research projects in the beginning stages, and when I told them about your experience in drafting on all the projects we've done together, they said you could come see what interests you." Dad smiled at Percy.

"No," said Percy. He looked Dad in the eye.

Dad frowned. "Well, if you're thinking of sailing, we need to talk. Your mother looked into a sailing club over in Santa Elena—and the prices were astronomical."

"I'm not thinking about sailing," said Percy, not adding that a sailing club was exactly what he'd been thinking of just a few hours ago. Sailing was pretty much a loner thing to do unless you were racing with a partner. But now that Christopher had told Percy that the ice cream girl worked at his camp he no longer wanted to do something all alone.

Dad frowned deeper. "What did you have in mind?"

"Something where I"—Percy hesitated—"stayed more with the family."

"I'm family," said Dad. "Look, if you want to stay close by me, I'll find you something to do on MOSE. You don't have to work with strangers."

Percy gave Mom a look that invited her to join the conversation.

Mom picked up the pamphlet about the Walker Evans photographic exhibit that she'd been talking about at dinner. She opened it, trying to look absorbed. She was the queen of avoidance.

"Look here," said Dad to Percy. He ran his index finger down the map along the southernmost island that closed off the lagoon. "The second floodgate will go at the Porto di Chioggia." He ran his finger back up to the north again. "And the third will go here, at the Porto di Lido. Once we've got all three areas fitted with floodgates, we can control the flow from the Adriatic into the lagoon."

Percy leaned over the map, interested in spite of himself. "But what about here? And here?" He pointed at the spaces between the other islands. "There are four islands blocking off the lagoon. That means there are five places for the Adriatic waters to flow in. But you're setting up floodgates at only three of them."

"Right." Dad smiled like the Cheshire cat in *Alice's Adventures in Wonderland*. "But the two northern islands are backed up by a series of smaller islands behind them." Dad hopped his finger around the map. "And these islands themselves act as a natural floodgate. With these three main channels controlled, there won't be any more flooding problems." He sat back and crossed his arms. "You asked exactly the right question, Percy. You're a natural at this. You'll enjoy the CNR. And it's much healthier than sitting around all day in the apartment. We have to get down to the actual physical work of putting the two other floodgates into place and you can help on that, certainly."

"Why do they need a civil engineer to put big machines in place? They can use anyone strong enough."

"Last-minute problems come up—adjustments to the machines might have to be made. I'm there to help figure out how to make those adjustments in the least costly and most effective way."

Percy nodded. "Sounds great, Dad. It really does." He thought of the ice cream girl's black eyes—like shiny olives. "But, uh, I think maybe I'd just be in the way."

"Nonsense. You're great at that kind of thing, Percy. You'll work right beside me." Dad smoothed the map flat, then folded it carefully.

Christopher came into the room in his pajamas. He sat

down in the middle of the living room floor and spread out his cards.

Percy mentally thanked Christopher for the timely appearance. "Maybe I should do things with other members of the family."

Mom looked up from her pamphlet. "You want to come with me while I draw?" She looked stunned.

Percy's eyes lighted on Christopher. "Maybe I should do something with Christopher."

"With Christopher?" Mom almost choked.

Dad shook his head. "I've already paid for him to be in this Estate Ragazzi camp at Don Bosco."

"And he likes the camp," said Mom. "He's staying in it."

"I thought maybe I'd go with him."

"It's for little children." Mom looked at Percy as if he were a half-wit. "I don't think you can even sign up if you're over twelve. They do children's activities all day. They make key cases out of leather and burn designs into wood with an electric soldering gun and I don't know what-all else."

"Filografia," said Christopher.

"And *filografia,*" said Mom. "Where'd you get those cards from, Christopher?"

"Percy bought them for me."

"I could be one of the *animatori,*" said Percy.

"The *animatori,*" repeated Mom.

"The counselors."

"I know what they are, Percy." Mom sighed. "You know I like to encourage you in whatever you want to do, but, honey . . ." She made a little *tsk*. "You don't speak Italian," she said in a gentle voice.

"I know."

"Well, how could you teach Italian children activities?"

"I can use my phrase book."

Mom didn't say anything.

"I could gesture. Italians understand gestures."

"How do you say, 'Please be quiet while I demonstrate,' using only gestures?"

Percy put his finger to his lips and said, "Shhh." Then he pointed to his chest and made exaggerated sewing motions in the air.

Mom pursed her lips.

Christopher clapped.

"What do you do when some kid babbles Italian and it turns out he was telling you he felt sick and then he vomits all over?"

Percy looked around. Christopher stared at him intently. "I'd clean up the vomit."

Christopher clapped.

"Look, Percy," said Mom, mustering her let's-be-reasonable tone, "they'd never take you. You'd just be in the way."

"They'd take you," said Christopher. "And she'd like you, too."

Mom looked bewildered. "Who'd like him?"

"The people there," said Percy quickly.

"Are you interested in a girl?" said Dad. "What happened to Vicky?"

"Vicky's not his girlfriend," said Christopher. "Vicky's his sailing partner."

"But she's cute," said Dad.

Percy raised his hands. "Enough, already. All I want to do is make friends with the other *animatori*."

"Chances are the other *animatori* don't speak English," said Mom. "If they did, they would have gotten well-paying jobs working somewhere that tourists go, rather than volunteering their time for the poor kids of Venice."

"Everyone studies English in school," said Percy, not knowing whether it was true and banking that his mother didn't know either.

"False. Everyone studies English or French or German. Italy has an agreement with the other countries of Europe that a certain percentage of its children will study European languages. Even if everyone wanted to study English, they couldn't."

"English is a European language," said Percy.

"Percy," said Mom in a warning tone.

There was something funny about the way Mom was stonewalling. "You know," said Percy, "it seems to me that you've got something else against my going there. Something you won't say."

Mom lifted her chin defiantly.

"I knew it," said Percy. "Look at her, Dad." Percy sat down across from his mother. "What's bothering you?"

"I don't feel up to trying to explain to the priests what you want to do," said Mom.

"You speak Italian great, Mom."

Mom shook her head. "I always feel strange when I talk to them. One of them asked if Christopher wanted to take confession." Mom shook her head again. "I'd rather not get into conversations with them."

"Mom, you don't owe them an apology because we're not Catholic."

"I know that," said Mom. "Don't patronize me, Percy."

"So what's the problem?"

"They don't know that."

"You don't have to come with me," said Percy. "I'll explain it myself."

"No you won't," said Dad. "You'll come with me, Percy."

"But, Dad—"

"Not another word about it. We'll get these two last floodgates in place and then we can work on the pollution problems of Venice."

Percy felt himself sink inside.

But Mom seemed to brighten at the opportunity to change the subject. She wrinkled her nose. "I just found out today that the sewers of Venice empty straight into the canals."

"Yuck!" The thought was enough to jerk Percy out of his depression. "That should be illegal."

"That's not a real problem," said Dad. "Raw sewage breaks down fast in running water and becomes harmless quickly."

"But the canals stink when it rains," said Mom. "Everyone says so."

"That's only because the city doesn't dredge them often enough. Anyway, the serious problem of Venice is industrial waste and agricultural pollution from the Po Valley."

"Insecticides," said Percy.

"And fertilizers. They heat up the waters of the Adriatic and cause algae. And the Adriatic is the deep-water source for the Mediterranean. If we change the temperature of the Adriatic—which is easy to do because it's so long and narrow—we threaten the ecology of the entire Mediterranean Sea."

"But if Italians know this, why don't they stop?" said Percy.

"They're trying to make a living. They won't think about the larger scale unless the government forces them by making it costly to pollute. Anyway, it isn't just the

Italians. The Greeks and the Egyptians are much worse offenders."

"The world's a mess," said Percy softly.

"I don't know if it's a mess," said Dad, standing up, "but it needs help." He stretched his arms over his head and yawned.

Percy put his elbows on the dining room table and let his face fall into his hands.

"Percy." Dad's voice was suddenly tender.

Percy looked up.

"You need something to do with yourself, as you said. Come with me tomorrow and we'll find things that will interest you. There're all sorts of challenges in this town."

"Could I walk Christopher to his program first?"

"Sure," said Dad. "That's a nice big-brotherly thing to do."

CHAPTER 6

"Lookit, lookit!" shouted Christopher. He ran ahead and stood near the bench under the tree beside the fountain in Campo Santa Margherita. A man in a blue uniform held a baby bird in his hands and peered up into the tree. He tossed the bird upward. It disappeared among the leaves, then came fluttering down again. Christopher scooped it up. The bird blinked and sat quietly in Christopher's hands. A black-and-white cat crouched under the bench and flicked his tail from side to side. The man in uniform pointed at the cat and said something to Christopher. Christopher placed the bird gently in Percy's hands. "Throw him, Percy. As high as you can. Or else he'll be cat food."

The bird was warm in Percy's hands. He weighed close

to nothing. A sparrow. Percy looked up into the branches. From about two thirds of the way up, an adult bird watched him. It would be impossible to throw the baby that high.

The man in uniform said, *"Forza."*

Percy took that for encouragement. He stood on the bench with his heart beating as hard as the bird's and threw as high as he could. The little bird was lost among the leaves for an instant.

"There he is!" Christopher pointed. "He's holding on."

The bird had alighted on a branch midway up. The adult bird watched. The cat came out from under the bench and sat, looking up at the baby bird. The man in uniform smiled and walked over toward the bank, where he took up his post as guard just inside the door. He waved. Percy waved back and took Christopher by the hand.

"You saved his life," said Christopher.

For now, thought Percy.

They bought the bread Mom wanted, dropped it off at home, and headed for camp. The way led past the train station and already at nine A.M. the tourists covered the steps and spilled over onto the small patch of grass beside the station. The vendors in the booths on both sides of the canal sold *gondoliere* hats and shirts as fast as the tourists could buy them.

"See." Christopher pointed under a table in an outdoor

cafe. Percy stooped over and looked. A brown-and-orange cat slept curled on the chair. "He's always there."

"He couldn't be. People must sit at that table sometime."

"He's always there," said Christopher again in a totally certain voice.

Percy and Christopher crossed the Scalzi Bridge. "This is the highest point in all Venice. Except in buildings."

Percy lifted an eyebrow. "What about the Rialto Bridge?"

"Nope. Here."

Percy smiled. He had to admire Christopher's certainty. It made his life easy.

They went down the busy Lista di Spagna, a sort of sleazy street that Mom said probably had the most overpriced stores in all Venice. But business was booming, especially in the open-air market.

"I want a banana," said Christopher as they watched a tall man with a backpack peel the one he'd just shelled out 2000 lire for. "But not here. Over past the Ponte delle Guglie they cost only five hundred lire." The man with the backpack looked at Christopher with dismay. Christopher ran on, pulling Percy by the hand and dodging tourists expertly. "That way." He pointed between a restaurant and a bookstore. "Down that alley is the entrance to the best park."

"A park in Venice? I thought there weren't any." Percy

looked hungrily in the direction Christopher had pointed. He missed the pleasure of walking barefoot on grass.

"I'll take you there Saturday if you want." Christopher pulled Percy over a big stone bridge. "Want to walk through the market or the ghetto?"

Percy felt disoriented by the fact that Christopher was so comfortable here, so obviously familiar with his surroundings. How did he learn so much so fast? "Uh . . . which is best?"

"We'll do both." Christopher wove his way through the crowd, which was now made up of old women pulling shopping carts and housewives with big cloth bags over their shoulders.

"Don't you hate liver beans?" said Christopher.

"Liver beans?" The name was discouraging. Percy looked across the piles of dried beans. "Which ones are liver beans?"

Christopher pointed. "Those, of course."

Percy smiled. "Those are kidney beans, jerko."

"Oh, yeah," said Christopher slowly, looking down in embarrassment.

Percy tousled Christopher's hair. His little brother didn't know everything, after all. "You were close. Livers are a lot like kidneys."

But Christopher had already run on to a fish counter. "See that one? Guess what he's called."

The fish was purple-brown with a wide, flat body. Not

flat up and down like a flounder, but flat sideways like a pancake. His jaw was the widest point. From above his mouth, just below his eyes, a long bony rod extended six or seven inches out. On the end of the rod was a hook-shaped blob of flesh that came to a ball at the tip. The body was bumpy and lumpy. Percy didn't think he'd ever seen such an ugly creature before. The fish vendor smiled at the boys. He opened the fish's mouth. It was gigantic, forming a gray squashy cave that exposed more than a third of the fish's insides. The teeth were many and sharp. With the mouth open like that, the flesh on the end of the rod bobbed as though it were alive.

"It's ugly," said Percy.

"It's a *pescatore*," said Christopher. "A fisherman. 'Cause it sits with its mouth open like that and little fish come along and see that junk hanging out front and think it's a worm and they latch on and the *pescatore* gobbles them up."

Percy shuddered.

The fish vendor let the fish's mouth drop closed and picked up a cleaver. He chopped off the fish's tail, slit the skin, slipped it off like a jacket, and held out the white meaty tail to Percy. *"Lo vuoi?"*

"No." Percy stepped back in alarm. *"No, grazie."*

The fish vendor laughed.

Christopher pulled a 500-lire piece out of his pocket and bought a banana at the next booth and kept on moving, pulling Percy. They passed a sign for a Chinese restaurant and Percy felt a flash of recognition. Suddenly they were back at the stone bridge where the market began and where they had stood only ten minutes ago. This time they headed along the side canal and darted into a tunnel.

"Hey, where are we going?" said Percy.

Christopher pulled Percy back out of the tunnel and pointed to the Hebrew words overhead. "This is the Jewish ghetto. Let's buy homemade matzoh. They make it all year long, just for the tourists." He dashed back inside the tunnel and Percy followed. When they came out, a kosher bakery faced them.

"Plain matzoh?" Percy stood firm at the doorway. "I like matzoh with butter and salt."

"Then let's wait till the way home," said Christopher reasonably. "We can buy it then and eat it at home the way you like."

"I won't be coming home with you," said Percy. "I can't stay. Dad expects me at the CNR."

Christopher stopped and looked at Percy accusingly.

"Oh, come on, you heard what Dad said last night."

"You're smart enough to get around Dad when you want to." Christopher walked ahead, crossed a little bridge at an ordinary pace, and made his way pensively across a deserted *campo*. "You'll miss all the fun." He chased half-heartedly through a group of pigeons. "I thought we could play together."

There was a sharp clank from one side of the *campo*. Percy turned and saw a wire trash basket balance on its rim for a moment before it settled. It was empty but for a can of black spray paint. Two people in overall shorts rounded the corner quickly. A light brown braid flashed out behind one. On the wall were big letters in black paint, the same letters Percy had seen a few days before on the wall near the prison: EXPO NO! He ran to the corner. No one was in sight.

"Was that Graziella?" he asked Christopher.

"I don't know. I didn't see them close enough."

Percy itched with frustration. This ice cream girl was so elusive, he was beginning to wonder if she was one girl or many or even if she was real at all. "Let's hurry up and get there, okay?"

Christopher took off without a word, out the far end of the *campo,* across a bridge and down the canal some three hundred yards. He turned in at a metal gate. Percy followed, expecting to find a ton of kids. But the small, dusty courtyard was empty.

"Where is everyone?"

"At church, across the canal." Christopher walked to a doorway at the end of the courtyard. "Sometimes I go, too. But usually I wait here."

Percy thought about Mom's reluctance to talk with the priests for fear questions of religion would come up.

"Does anyone ever bother you 'cause you don't go to church?"

"No one can bother me. All I have to do is pretend I don't understand what they're saying." Christopher gave a sly smile. "Anyway, the priests don't really care what I do as long as I act nice." He went through the doorway, calling over his shoulder. "Come on in, the *animatori* are setting up."

Percy felt his throat tighten. He peeked cautiously.

"Are you the brother of Christopher?" said a heavily accented male voice. A hand stretched out and Percy looked into the clean-shaven face of a man who must have been about twenty and who was a head shorter than Percy. The sensation was odd—Percy was used to being among the smallest guys back home. "Welcome. I'm Alessandro." He wore overall shorts.

"Hello. I'm Percy." Percy smiled and looked past Alessandro. At one of the long folding tables sat the ice cream girl. She looked at him expectantly and her eyes smiled hello. Her dimples were as deep as ever. Her hands were in her big pockets. Her legs were folded under her and one strap of her overall shorts fell loosely to the side. The T-shirt underneath was a pale yellow and Percy imagined for a moment that she tasted like sugared lemons. Christopher sat down beside her and counted out nails from a box, putting them into piles.

Alessandro stepped back and motioned for Percy to come in. He looked with open curiosity from Percy to Graziella. "You have met Graziella?"

"*Sì,*" said Percy. "*Ciao,* Graziella."

"*Ciao.*" Graziella didn't get up and made no motion to invite Percy closer. But her eyes were interested. She gave the impression of being shy. And suddenly shyness seemed desirable—and inviting.

Percy swallowed his tension. He wanted to talk. Make friends. He turned to Alessandro. "What's Expo?"

Alessandro lifted his chin and his eyes became wary. Graziella got up immediately and came to his side. With her hands in her pockets and his back so stiff, they looked as if they were in the military, standing at attention. Percy fought the urge to take a step backward.

"Expo means expo," said Alessandro quietly. "It's the same in English. A world fair, no?—all the nations display their products."

"Oh, of course." Percy flushed. Graziella's eyes were fixed on him, as if daring him. Well, Percy could certainly meet a dare. "Why did you paint 'Expo no' on the wall?"

"Wall?" Alessandro's face went blank—purposely, Percy was sure.

Did Alessandro think Percy was stupid? "The wall in the ghetto *campo.*"

Graziella moved closer to Alessandro until their arms

touched. Alessandro smiled coldly. "You make a mistake. I painted nothing."

The whole situation suddenly seemed dramatic in a silly way. Here were two young Italian people acting as though Percy had invaded some private world. As though he were treading on dangerous territory. There was something indirect and strange about their behavior. Something un-American. Normally Percy would have shut up and gone his own way. But he didn't have to act normal. He didn't want to act normal. He plowed on recklessly. "But you both did. I saw you."

"You make a mistake. I have to get out my materials now. The children will be coming back from church soon. You may leave." Alessandro went to the cupboard and put a stack of sheets of leather on the table nearest him. He didn't look at Percy.

Graziella went to the table and sat down beside Christopher. She turned her back squarely to Percy.

Christopher looked at Percy with big eyes. Then he did the most remarkable thing: He fell sideways off the bench.

Graziella jumped to Christopher's aid. She pulled Christopher up. There was black paint on the thumb and index finger of her right hand. Christopher threw his arms around Graziella's neck as she hugged him to her. He stared past her cheek at Percy.

Percy nodded and left.

He went blindly back through the ghetto *campo,* not even stopping to look at the painted letters on the wall. By the time he got to the boat stop, he was running. Clearly he had made a terrible gaffe. It was illegal to paint on walls, that was so in any city. But Percy wasn't an officer of the law; why should Alessandro and Graziella lie to him? And why did Graziella pretend she didn't speak English when she obviously understood everything Percy said? And why did they care about a world's fair? And when had Christopher grown up so much?

Percy flashed his Carta Venezia, the little identity card for residents that let him get on the boats at a reduced price, bought a ticket, and got onto the number 52 boat for the Fondamenta Nuove. The boat was practically empty. He sat down near a window and looked out at the Canale di Cannaregio and then at the lagoon. The morning sun sparkled off the buildings, off the water, off the bridge. Everything seemed peaceful and perfect. Again Percy got that strange feeling of being deceived. He half expected a disaster—the boat to turn over or someone to shout, "Fire!" But nothing happened. The sun still shone.

A small sense of calm gradually returned to him. He looked up at the miniature billboards that circled the walls above the windows. One was in Italian with some Asian characters across the bottom. He thought of the sign for the Chinese restaurant that he and Christopher had passed in the market. Below the characters someone had painted the English words: MEN DON'T PROTECT YOU ANYMORE. Percy felt taken aback. Overt feminism in Italy surprised him a little. Oh, he didn't believe the stupid remarks that Italian men were all fabulous lovers and Italian women were all beautiful baby machines. Mom had read him the statistics before they came—about how there had been a higher percentage of women in medical school in Italy twenty years ago than there was in America today—things like that. But he still found Italian women somewhat— what?—genteel, maybe. And definitely beautiful. Just about every young girl he passed wore spandex and moved in a way that made him look twice. They were hot.

He thought of Graziella's delicate features. It was hard to imagine her being strident. Yet at the camp her eyes had been cold. And there was no denying it—the message on the billboard was direct: Women in Venice were angry.

And Alessandro and Graziella were angry about something else—this Expo business—this thing they had to say no to with black paint.

Percy closed his eyes and let himself feel the movement of the boat. When he was in elementary school, one of his best friends, Anthony More, had been blind. Percy had taken on the job of making sure Anthony got on the right bus after school. He formed the habit of sitting beside Anthony on the bus with his eyes closed, so that they'd be having the same experience, just talking. It calmed Percy in a strange way. Then Anthony's family moved away

CHAPTER 7

Percy followed Dad's engineer friends around the CNR, nodding respectfully when anyone spoke to him, but he couldn't focus on what they said. His eyes kept seeing pale yellow; his nose kept smelling lemon; the palms of his hands itched to touch a long smooth braid. When they finished at lunchtime, Percy felt a tension inside release.

"Do you like the beach?" asked Paolo as Dad and Percy stood beside him in the line for the boat home.

"Sure."

"Last summer he was a lifeguard," said Dad proudly.

"A lifeguard?" Paolo looked impressed. "Then you had better pass as many days as possible at the Lido now, because with this heat, by the middle of the month the

71

waters will be full of—I do not know the English word—the *mucillagine*."

"Mucilage," said Dad. He smiled at Percy. "Slime."

Yuck, thought Percy.

Dad and Percy got off at their boat stop. They wound their way through the alleys and crossed Campo Santa Margherita. The bank guard stood under the tree where Percy had rescued the little bird that morning. Percy called out, *"Buon giorno, Signore."* He waved.

The guard grinned. *"Salve."* He pointed up into the leaves. Percy looked. The little bird had moved to a higher branch.

"How do you know him?" asked Dad as they hurried on.

"We sort of rescued a baby bird together this morning." Percy laughed. "I wonder if he's been standing out here keeping watch over it."

"Probably he has nothing better to do," said Dad. "No one's about to rob this tiny bank branch. The bird may have been the great excitement of his day. Maybe of his week."

Percy looked back over his shoulder at the figure in blue, standing patiently under the tree. He hoped the man would stand there all day. He hoped he would become the guardian of all the birds in the *campo*.

"You know, Dad . . ." Percy hesitated. "Thanks for

taking me this morning and all, but I don't think I'll come along this afternoon."

Dad stopped in his tracks. He picked at his teeth and looked at Percy. "It's an important project, Percy. The city floods almost every year. You'll find people who will tell you that high waters come only in November, but it's not true. They can come anytime. The bora can strike even in summer, though I admit that's rare."

"What's the bora?"

"The cold wind that comes down from Trieste. And the hot wind from the south is called the scirocco. When the storms hit, usually the waters rise over the canals and enter the bottom level of the buildings just a little bit. But now and then a major flood comes and people paddle boats through the *campos*."

"It must be a mess," Percy said halfheartedly.

"It's more than a mess. The water supply gets contaminated and people get sick. Great pieces of art get ruined. MOSE is important, Percy."

"I know, Dad. I respect what you're doing. That's not the point."

Dad looked at Percy thoughtfully. "You need fun. How about we grab our swimsuits and get on a boat out to the Lido?"

"I thought you were supposed to meet everyone at the Porto di Malamocco this afternoon?"

"I will. After we spend a little time at the beach."

"Okay."

Within the hour Percy and Dad arrived at the beach called the Blue Moon. It was a public beach with what turned out to be a decent cafeteria. They sat in extreme pleasure over a pizza that had been baked in a wood-burning oven with four kinds of cheeses on it, washed down with an ice-cold Coke.

"I like Italian food," said Percy in a tone that bordered on reverence.

"Who doesn't?" said Dad.

Percy leaned back and looked out the window at the beach. "There's a poor excuse for a soccer game down there."

Dad followed Percy's eyes to the edge of the water. "You want to join them?"

Percy gave a small laugh. "It's kind of tough to go up and intrude on a game like that."

"Yeah." Dad wiped his mouth. "You're bored with us, with Paolo and Marina and me. You need to be with people your own age."

"That's what I was trying to tell you."

Dad slumped slightly. "I suppose I could spring for the sailing club. After all, you need to have fun."

"I really don't want to sail here, Dad. Really."

Dad looked confused and relieved at the same time. He sat up straighter. "Maybe you should find a job. I can pick up a copy of the *Gazzettino* and you can get your mother to help you make calls."

A job. The only kind of job Percy could do was one where he'd speak English all day—a job with tourists. But it wasn't tourists he wanted to get to know. "Tell me, what's all this about Expo?" he asked as though the thought had just popped into his head.

"Expo?" Dad looked blank.

For a minute Percy was afraid his father, the great source of all information, was going to fail him. "You know, the world's fair."

"Oh, yes, Expo."

"So what's up?" said Percy. "What's it got to do with Venice?"

"The city council has proposed to host the next world's fair. The question is where the money is going to come from to set it up."

"What's to set up?" asked Percy.

"It's a big deal—very expensive. They've proposed taking an entire island north of Venice and turning it into the pavilion for the exhibits. They'd build a huge amusement park and concession stands and the whole bit."

"All that just for a world's fair?"

Dad raised an eyebrow. "Millions of people come to a world's fair. It's big business."

"What happens to it all after the fair?"

"The place would become a permanent amusement

park." Dad put money on the table and got up. Percy followed. "The park would attract even more tourists to Venice, and the city would be that much richer, or so the theory goes." Dad snorted.

"But you don't believe that?"

"Look, Percy, the city can't handle all the waste and garbage produced by the tourists now. What do you think will happen if the number of tourists goes up even ten percent? And think of the year of the Expo. There will be millions of extra people tramping through Venice."

"So why do the Venetians want to do it?"

"You can answer that yourself."

"To make money." Percy put his toes under a crushed paper cup and flipped it up into his hand. He dropped it in the nearby trash can. "The farmers in the Po Valley and now the merchants of Venice."

"Yup. That's the cause of the mucilage, by the way. All the fertilizer runoff from the Po Valley."

Percy shook his head. "The whole world is going down the toilet because of greed."

"With the right actions soon, we can still turn things around."

Percy thought about Graziella and Alessandro and their cans of spray paint. "Do you think people will take the right actions?"

Dad put his arm tightly around Percy's shoulders. "We

have to work for what we believe in, Percy. And then . . ."

"Then?"

"Then we've got to hope others do the same."

Graziella was working for something she clearly believed in. "I want to go to Christopher's camp tomorrow."

Dad shook his head. "I don't know if Christopher's camp is the answer to your loneliness."

No, it probably isn't, thought Percy. Even though he hated to admit it, it looked painfully obvious that Graziella wasn't interested in knowing Percy. But, no. That kind of giving up was the attitude of the old Percy—the Percy back home, who never pushed ahead on anything that had to do with girls. This was his summer of transformation. "I think I'll give it a try, though."

"Sure. It can't hurt."

CHAPTER 8

"Voglio fare animatore," said Percy, carefully pronouncing every letter on the sheet of paper that he'd written that crucial sentence on.

Don Mario, the priest in charge of the whole Estate Ragazzi, nodded thoughtfully. *"Potresti insegnare qualcosa?"*

Oh, no, what had he said? Percy pulled his dictionary out of his hip pocket and looked up the word *insegnare:* "to teach." Oh, okay, he was asking if Percy could teach the activities. That's what the *animatori* did. Well . . . no. Percy didn't know the first thing about making leather goods or that crazy *filografia* with the nails and string. But how hard could it be?

Christopher came into the room, pulling Alessandro by the hand. "I brought a translator."

Alessandro looked at Percy without expression. He extended his hand. Percy took it and shook. "How can I help?" asked Alessandro.

"I want to be a counselor. An *animatore*," said Percy. "Like you."

Alessandro's eyes showed no reaction. He spoke with Don Mario in quiet, fast Italian. Then he turned to Percy. "Can you teach anything?"

Percy ran his tongue across inside his top lip.

"He can run sports," said Christopher. "He's great at soccer."

"Great at soccer?" Alessandro showed a hint of a smile. "Really?"

"I'm okay," said Percy.

Alessandro talked with Don Mario. "Stay today. Help out however you can this morning. Then in the afternoon we'll see what you can do on the soccer field."

Percy nodded. He held out his hand to Don Mario. *"Grazie."*

Don Mario shook Percy's hand. *"Benvenuto."*

Alessandro was already out the door and Christopher tagged behind him. Percy caught up. "Where do I start?"

"Wherever you can be of use." Alessandro went into the room where Percy had met him yesterday.

Percy followed. The room couldn't have been more than ten feet by fifteen feet, but Percy would have sworn it held at least fifty kids, mostly on benches at the long tables, but some in groups on the floor. Graziella sat at a table and helped a boy hammer nails into a board. He looked like the youngest kid in the room. She didn't so much as glance at Percy but he was sure she knew he was there. She had on blue-and-white-striped pants, the ones Percy thought he had seen her in Monday on the bridge behind the prison. Her braid was fastened at the bottom with some odd-shaped silver clip. Percy wanted a closer look at the clip, but he didn't dare yet. He checked his dictionary, then went over to her and said slowly, *"Posso aiutare il bambino,"* which meant, if the dictionary was right, "I can help the child."

Graziella looked at him with surprise. Then her expression softened. He almost thought for a moment that she would smile. She got up and motioned to Percy to take her place. *"Allora,"* she said, *"forza."*

Forza. That's what the bank guard had said when Percy had stood with the baby bird in his hands. It was a friendly word of encouragement. At least, Percy would take it as one. He gave Graziella a big smile and turned to the boy, who stared at him and at the same time lifted his hammer and swung without looking down. The boy smashed his finger and the nail flew off the table. Percy had been on the job less than two seconds and already he had a casualty. He prepared for the scream, but instead the boy's eyes filled with tears and he quietly sucked his sore thumb and rocked back and forth. Percy was overcome with sympathy and at the same time gratitude that the boy hadn't screamed and called everyone's attention to what a bad job he was doing as a caretaker. He put one leg over the bench and swung the other leg around the boy, moving carefully so that he wouldn't kick any of the other kids. When he was straddling the boy, he scooped him up onto his lap and rocked with him, stroking his hair. The boy leaned against Percy's chest and looked up at him with wide eyes. Percy held him closer. From across the table a girl about ten years old watched Percy with curiosity. He smiled at her and she immediately picked up her hammer and pounded away wildly, keeping her eyes averted.

Percy took a nail from the pile on the table and held it firm just as the boy had before he'd smashed his finger. He handed the hammer to the boy, who took it, and, with his eyes still on Percy's face, promptly smashed Percy's thumb. Wow, it hurt. Percy put his thumb in his mouth and rocked back and forth with the little boy on his lap.

The boy looked frightened. He whispered, *"Mi dispiace."*

Percy patted the boy on the head to show he accepted the apology. What was a little pain? If the boy could go on living with a smashed thumb, so could Percy. He took the boy's face between his palms and directed it so that the boy had to look at the creation he was making. Then he put the hammer in the boy's hand and quickly put his own right hand over the boy's. He held the nail in place with the second and third fingers of his left hand (his thumb still throbbed) and directed the boy's hammer down onto the nail. They got it in. Then they did the same to another nail. And another.

Gradually they formed a shape that seemed to satisfy the boy, who hummed tunelessly. The boy put down the hammer and pointed to the spools of colored string. *"Rosso."*

Yeah, that was red. Percy had studied the color words last night. They wound the red string from nail to nail in a pattern the boy seemed very sure of. It reminded Percy of a bleeding penguin.

A bell rang. Instantly kids dropped hammers into piles in the center of the tables and lined up their unfinished creations on the shelves. The little boy hopped off Percy's lap and followed suit. Percy watched him go with a twinge of sadness. The boy didn't wave goodbye.

Graziella moved quickly from spot to spot along the tables, leaving little piles of nails for the next group of children. Percy thought of offering to help, but something about her manner stopped him. She was too busy and brusque to be bothered with him right now.

Percy wandered across a corridor into a smaller room. A skinny sandy-haired *animatore* sat on a bar stool with a guitar slung across his chest. One foot was hooked onto the bottom rung of the stool. The other foot swung easily. A dozen or more kids took their places on the floor in front of him. Percy backed out quietly and went into the next room, which was larger and had tables like the first room, but these were covered with scraps of leather and tools that resembled X-acto knives. Christopher ran in past Percy with a quick smile, got a sack off one of the shelves, and dumped it onto a table. Then he sat down and set to work on his leather.

Among the other children already seated was Percy's own little boy. He clutched his sack and seemed distracted. Percy couldn't imagine his boy handling one of those knives. A tall blond girl sat down beside him and emptied his bag for him. The boy let his hands fall limp to his sides.

Percy left and traveled down the corridor to the last room. About twenty twelve-year-old boys worked at constructing an electric circuit to what Percy figured out was a doorbell. This was clearly the spot for the big boys' activity. And this was something he could help at. Percy had built dozens of electric circuits for his Principles of Technology course—what everyone called POT. He went into the room and stood against the wall to watch the social dynamics of the boys first. You could plow right in with little kids, but not with big ones. They talked quickly, punched each other in the shoulder, argued over where to connect what. One of the boys took the leader's role and made the decision. He was right—he fit the wire just where it should go.

Percy thought he'd walk over for a closer look, but he

found himself turning around. He went back to the room with the leather. His little boy looked out the window onto the empty, dusty playing court while the tall blond girl worked away at his leather with a knife. Percy tapped the boy on the shoulder. *"Ciao."*

The boy looked up. A slow smile crossed his face. He put his thumb in his mouth for a moment.

Percy laughed. *"Va bene ora,"* he said, hoping he remembered his phrase book correctly and this meant, "It's okay now." He sucked his own thumb for a second, then pulled it out of his mouth and showed it to the boy. *"Va bene. Va bene."*

The boy took Percy's thumb and pulled him down on the bench, at the same time pushing the blond girl away.

The girl looked at Percy and smiled. *"Vuoi aiutarlo?"*

"Non capisco," said Percy, which he knew meant "I don't understand." That was one phrase he'd practiced with Mom.

The girl stood up and stepped away from the bench. Percy sat down. His little boy climbed onto his lap and picked up the knife. The blond girl grabbed it from him. *"Va bene,"* said Percy soothingly to the girl. He took the knife from her and put it back in the boy's hand. He put his own hand over the boy's. The girl watched with a critical look. *"Va bene,"* said Percy with more assurance. He turned his back to the girl, and she finally walked away. Percy moved the leather close to the boy and held it in place with his left hand. Together and painstakingly, Percy and the boy cut an irregular but recognizable rectangle. Then they put it through a metal ring and stood in line to use the machine that put brads through the leather. By the end of the activity period, the boy held his key ring tight in his right hand and Percy's hand even tighter in his left.

Christopher and Percy walked home for lunch, with Christopher talking a mile a minute about all the things he'd done that morning. He reminded Percy of a happy bird, chirping like mad. Percy stopped listening and let himself enjoy a sense of peace. Nothing had happened that morning, really. But it had been a good morning, all the same. Percy had been useful. And he liked his own little boy.

Mom came out the gate as they arrived, her camera and equipment sticking out of the cloth bag over her shoulder. "Oh, there you are, boys. I'm so glad I got to see you before I left. I'm on my way to Suzy's—"

"Suzy?" interrupted Percy.

"That American I told you about. The one who married the *gondoliere*. She has a friend, a very old woman, who's going to let me photograph her. Then I'll paint her portrait from the photographs. She's a lace-maker who grew up on Burano, and she's almost blind from working all her life on lace, and—"

"She's blind from working?" said Christopher with horror on his face.

"Yes. It's awful. That kind of intricate work ruins your eyes. But apparently she loves the work. She does it still; her hands do it automatically. I can't wait to see what she looks like. I bet she has an expressive face." Mom sighed dreamily. Then she smiled at the boys. "I left you tuna sandwiches on the table."

"I hate tuna," said Christopher.

"It's all I had," said Mom. "Percy, get him to eat, okay? All of it, please. How'd your morning go?"

"Fine." Percy nodded with his head and shoulders together.

"Good. I want to hear all about it later. I'll meet you here at four, as usual. We're going to a terrific museum. Bye now." She kissed them both and ran.

Percy followed Christopher upstairs.

"I'm not eating," said Christopher, "no matter what you do. I hate tuna." He rummaged through the refrigerator. "There's nothing to eat," he moaned. "Nothing else at all."

Percy opened the cupboard and reached up to the top shelf. He pulled out an unopened bag of M&M's. "Okay, Christopher, here's the story. You eat half your sandwich and I'll let you get sick on candy."

Christopher sat at the table. "Half?"

"Half," said Percy.

Christopher took a bite. Percy poured two glasses of

milk, dropped the bag of candy in the center of the table, and sat down. He ate his sandwich and Christopher ate his, keeping his eyes on the candy. "I made a key ring today," said Christopher.

Percy washed down his last bite of sandwich with the rest of the milk. "Yeah, I made one with a kid, too."

"But yours was simple," said Christopher, "because Matteo has no brains."

"What?"

"That's what they say. He's Chinese or something."

"I take it my little boy's name is Matteo?"

"Right," said Christopher. "I saw the key ring he made. Mine is nicer. But he has the best kind of backpack. I want one like his. We're supposed to have backpacks so we can take home the things we make at Don Bosco." He wiped his mouth on his arm. "And, look, I finished half the sandwich, so I get the M&M's." He reached for the bag.

Percy pulled the bag away.

"No fair!" shouted Christopher. "I ate half and you said—"

"You ate the wrong half."

Christopher's face went blank. "Oh." He picked up the remaining half sandwich and ate.

Percy watched Christopher in amazement. Sometimes his brother seemed so smart and sometimes he was so dumb. "Who told you Matteo was Chinese?"

"Graziella."

"That's ridiculous," said Percy. "Matteo's not Chinese."

"Then he's something else. Something from far away. Mongolian or something."

"Mongoloid," said Percy slowly.

"That's it. That's why he's got no brains."

"Is that how Graziella said it?" asked Percy.

"I don't know," said Christopher. "I don't know exactly what she said. But I understood what she meant. She pointed at his head and explained so I wouldn't expect things from him. Everyone's supposed to look out for him. He's ten."

"Ten!" Percy remembered how light Matteo had felt on his lap. "He's smaller than you."

"And he gets colds all the time. And he always needs help. The *animatori* are sick of him."

"Who told you that?"

"I figured it out. They argue each morning over who's going to take care of him during the activities. No one wants to."

"Well, they don't have to argue anymore," said Percy. "I want to."

Christopher swallowed his last bite of sandwich. "See? I finished. Give me the M&M's."

Percy passed the bag to him.

CHAPTER 9

Percy squeezed the last drop of juice out of his wedge of lemon. It mixed with the olive oil left on his plate from the tomato salad. He licked the plate.

"Here," said Dad. He handed Percy a ripped-off chunk of bread. Then he mopped his own plate with bread.

Percy set the bread down and licked the plate again.

"Come on, Percy," said Mom. "Don't act like a pig."

Percy snuffled his nose against his plate and grunted.

"Oink, oink, oink," shouted Christopher. "We're pigs. *Oink, oink, oink."* He licked the piece of chicken breast on his plate.

"Pigs can wash the dishes tonight," said Mom.

"Pretty good on the uptake, Mom, got to hand it to you." Percy carried his dishes to the sink.

"You're happy." Mom placed her dishes on the counter. "And you hummed your way through the Accademia museum this afternoon." She smiled. "I take it the Estate Ragazzi camp was fun?"

"It was all right." Percy set the washed plate and glass on the drainer, which was mounted on the wall high up over the sink. It was a nifty system: The dishes dripped into the sink. They should do that in America.

Christopher stabbed his chicken breast repeatedly with his fork. "Percy umpired the soccer game I was in."

"Refereed, not umpired," said Percy.

Christopher spoke with a full mouth. "Refereed. He was great."

"Oh, yeah?" Dad slapped Percy on the shoulder. "They're accepting you, huh?"

"Sort of, I guess," said Percy. "How'd the progress go on the floodgate?"

Dad put things away in the refrigerator. "I think the whole thing will be in place within days. Anyone want to watch a soccer match with me on TV?"

"I'll watch with you." Christopher put his plate on the counter.

"You've hardly eaten," said Mom.

"I'm not hungry," said Christopher.

"I thought you were going with me to get ice cream," said Percy.

"I'd rather watch TV."

"Then you have to wash dishes with me, because you're a pig, too," said Percy.

"And if I go get ice cream with you, I don't have to wash dishes?" said Christopher.

"Right," said Percy.

"Then I want ice cream," said Christopher. "Sorry, Dad, I'll watch TV with you later."

Dad went into the living room with his newspaper.

"How can you want ice cream when you weren't hungry enough to finish your chicken?" Mom wiped the table as she talked.

"Huh?" said Christopher.

"Contradiction," said Mom. She put Christopher's plate back on the table and steered him toward it. "Finish the chicken, or no ice cream."

Christopher sighed as he ate. "You don't need me, you know, Percy. You can go to the *gelateria* all on your own."

Percy was thrown for a second by Christopher's use of the Italian word for "ice cream store." It had come so easily out of Christopher's mouth. But now that Percy was part of the Estate Ragazzi, maybe Italian words would start flowing out of his mouth, too. Yeah. "You're coming to the *gelateria* with me."

"I swear you can do it alone," said Christopher.

"You're coming with me," said Percy.

"I want to do things to my new backpack." Christopher got up and went to the plastic sack on the counter. He took out the backpack Mom had bought him on the way home from the museum. He touched each zipper lovingly.

Percy watched him, puzzled. "What's to do to a backpack?"

"Well, see, this pocket here is just the right size for a tank." Christopher unzipped it. "And this one is good for Pongo, and . . ."

"What's Pongo?"

"That clay Mom bought me."

Percy picked the pan off the stove and put it in the sink. "You can fill the pockets with junk later. For now, you're coming with me."

"Why are you so afraid of her?" said Christopher.

"Her?" said Mom.

Percy gave Christopher a sharp look and turned back to the sink. He ran the hot water over the pan.

"Who's her?" said Mom.

Christopher looked confused. "Don't you mean, 'Who's she?'? Percy's always correcting me about things like that."

"Percy's right," said Mom, "who is she?"

"No one," said Percy. "Sit down and finish your chicken, Christopher, and stop blabbing."

"Oh, how nice," said Mom. "Percy's interested in someone, is he, Christopher?"

"Out, Mother!" Percy pushed his mom out the kitchen door.

"Okay," Mom called back. "I'll just take a hot bath and then read the mail and you can tell me all about your adventures when you get home."

Percy looked threateningly at Christopher.

Christopher gobbled chicken.

The *campo* was lively by eight-thirty. Back home Christopher was in bed at eight-thirty, but in the week that they'd been in Venice the family had come around to European hours. Dinner was later, bedtime was later, waking was later. Percy watched the excitement in Christopher's face. When Christopher squeezed Percy's hand, Percy squeezed back protectively.

The *gelateria* was open and Percy had guessed right; this was Graziella's weekend job. She had on her blue-and-white-striped pants, the kind worn by almost every fifth person he passed on the streets. But no one looked better in them than Graziella. Percy waited till there was no one at the outside counter and no one inside, either. Then he stepped in. *"Ciao."*

The corners of Graziella's mouth turned up in a slight, formal smile, but her eyes betrayed her: They were warm and friendly. *"Ciao."*

Christopher ran to the counter. *"Una coppetta di banana e cioccolato, per favore."*

Graziella filled a little cup with a scoop of banana ice cream and a scoop of chocolate. She stuck in a yellow plastic spoon and handed it to Christopher.

"Grazie," said Christopher.

"Prego." Graziella looked at Percy expectantly.

This was his big moment. No peach ice cream this time. *"Un cono di stracciatella,"* said Percy carefully and loudly, pointing at the chocolate chip for good measure.

Graziella smiled broadly. *"Sì, signore, subito."* She came out from behind the counter and went to a freezer with a glass door. There were all sorts of fancy desserts inside. Graziella took out what looked like a fat ice cream sandwich, wrapped it in a napkin, and handed it to Percy.

Percy looked at the thing in his hand. The outside was a thin light brown cookie. The inside was an inch thick of frozen whipped cream. He took a bite. It was fabulous. He looked at Graziella, who was watching him from behind the counter now, her eyes sparkling with suppressed laughter. He nodded, grinned, and took another bite. *"Quanto?"* he asked.

"Tre mila."

Three thousand lire. Okay. Percy took out a 5,000-lire bill and handed it to Graziella. *"Per stasera e per l'altra sera,"* he said, having rehearsed the line many times. It meant, "for tonight and for the other night."

Graziella put the money in the cash register and set the change on the counter. *"Grazie."*

Percy looked around. Christopher had gone outside and stood with his back toward them, watching children play ball. Percy looked at Graziella again as he took another bite of his whipped-cream sandwich. She looked back with steady eyes. Percy turned and examined the things inside the glass freezer. There were frozen fruits, split and stuffed with ice cream: lemons, oranges, cantaloupes, kiwis, bananas, strawberries. There were layer cakes six inches high that looked as if they hardly weighed five ounces; they were all whipped egg whites and cream. There were large balls of chocolate that Percy guessed must be filled with cake or ice cream or both. And every dessert was beautiful—a work of art. Percy finished off his whipped cream and looked at Graziella again. She watched him.

A group of young men came into the store. Graziella served them cheerfully, seeming to know most of them. Percy stood against the back wall. He figured he'd leave when they left. But when they left, he still stood there and Graziella returned his unblinking look. Two middle-aged couples came in and ordered *tartufi*. Graziella filled a box with six of the chocolate balls Percy had been studying before. She wrapped it in colored paper and added a bow. They left. Percy moved up to the counter, pulling his worn dictionary from his pocket. He had decided the phrase book didn't have the phrases he wanted, so he'd left it at home. Anyway, he'd been studying the most-used verbs. Between those verbs and the dictionary he should

Graziella nodded.

Percy smiled and half ran from the store. Christopher was now over near a pile of trash behind the fountain. Percy grabbed his brother around the waist and lifted him up. "Hi, kiddo."

Christopher laughed. "What did she say?"

Percy laughed back. "How'd you get so smart?"

"I watch things," said Christopher.

"Oh yeah? Like what?"

"Anything. People mostly."

"All people?" asked Percy.

"Sure," said Christopher. "And if they catch me watching, they sometimes talk to me and make friends."

"Were you watching us in the ice cream store?"

"No. Look." Christopher pulled Percy over to the trash pile he had been staring at. He pointed and spoke in an awed voice. "A hypergermic needle."

Percy looked at the syringe and shivered. "It's 'derm,' not 'germ': a hypodermic."

"Hyperdermic?" said Christopher. "But it's got germs."

"Yeah, bad ones. Never touch one, you hear?"

"I know that," said Christopher. "Everyone knows that." He ran off toward home.

Percy picked a dirty envelope from the pile of trash and scooped up the syringe with it, careful not to touch it. He slid them both into the garbage can in the *campo*. Then he followed his brother slowly home. When he opened the apartment door, he saw his mother sitting on the couch, looking depressed, with his father's arm around her. Even Christopher, who sat on the floor at his mother's feet, looked subdued. "Who died?" Percy asked.

"I got a mean letter," said Mom. She pointed to a crumpled piece of paper on the floor.

Percy picked it up. It was in Italian. "So what's it say?"

"It says we should use those awful plastic bags for our garbage." Mom sobbed a little. "It says that we're terrible foreigners because we're guests in this pretty city and we're making everything awful by putting our garbage in paper bags that the dogs rip up." Mom sobbed a little harder. "It says that the neighborhood is angry at us and that they've taken photographs of our garbage to send to all the newspapers."

"Huh?" Percy looked at the letter. "What newspaper in its right mind would want to print a photograph of our garbage?"

Dad smothered a small laugh and looked out the window.

"Don't act smart about this, young man," sobbed Mom, really getting into it now. "And don't you support him, Vince," she said to Dad.

"Look, with all the dog turds all over the place,

they have no right to complain about our garbage," said Percy.

Mom shook her head and wailed, "They think we're awful."

"Well, they're stupid," said Percy. "Plastic is terrible for the environment. No one should put their garbage in plastic bags."

"I know that," said Mom irritably. "You don't have to lecture me. Why do you think I use paper, anyway?"

"Okay, okay," said Dad. "That's enough of that. We'll solve this the easy way. Instead of putting out our garbage for the garbagemen to pick up every morning, we can put it in little sacks, paper sacks," he added, looking swiftly at Mom, "and I'll dump it in the public garbage cans in the *campo* on my way to work."

Everyone looked at Mom.

"All right," Mom said finally. "But maybe we should write them a little note back explaining why we use paper bags."

Percy looked the letter over on both sides. "How can you write back? It's unsigned."

"They said it was a group of neighbors. I could post an answer on our front gate."

"It wasn't the neighbors," said Christopher.

"What?" said Mom.

"It was the garbagemen."

"Oh," said Mom slowly.

"How do you know?" asked Dad. "How would the garbagemen know we were foreigners?"

"I told them," said Christopher.

"You did?" said Mom.

"Yeah. We're friends. And today I saw them put the letter in the mailbox, but I didn't know what it was about."

"Oh, dear," said Mom. "It's another one of those cases of when in Rome . . ." She sighed.

"You should feel better," said Dad. "At least you know the neighborhood isn't up in arms about our garbage."

"It's so unfair," said Mom, "because I've been trying so hard to fit in. I bought Christopher those shoes that all the other kids wear, and the backpack he wanted. And I bought Percy those blue-striped pants . . ."

"What pants?" said Percy.

"The ones I put on your bed. I bought them at the market at Sacca Fisola today. Only thirteen thousand lire. All the young people wear them."

Percy ran into his and Christopher's room. On his bed were pants just like the ones Graziella was wearing right now. Should he put them on? Would they look like twins? But Graziella and Alessandro had worn the same overall shorts yesterday, so she didn't have anything against wearing the same clothes as the guy she was with. And tonight Percy was the guy she would be with.

And where would Alessandro be tonight?

Maybe Percy could pass for Venetian in these pants. But he wasn't Venetian. And Graziella knew that. He puffed up his cheeks and blew out the air slowly. Too bad Christopher had to go to bed. Percy would have to face Graziella alone, in striped pants, brand new, no less.

CHAPTER 10

Percy stood outside the *gelateria* with a growing sense of desperation. From across the *campo* he had watched Graziella close up the awning and go inside, shutting the door behind her. By the time he reached the door, it was locked. He looked at his watch. It was only ten forty-five. He wished there were a window he could peek in. It was impossible to tell if there was even a light on inside. He walked back and forth in front of the store.

Night fell late here, but it fell swiftly. The sky turned from dark gray to almost black in a matter of minutes. Early last fall Percy had gone sailing at night with Vicky— only once, but it had been marvelous. Out on the water the night sky had been this dark. But other than that, Percy had never known a night as dark as the nights in Venice. This city had few street lamps and the ones it had gave off feeble light, so nothing interfered with the blackness of the heavens.

Percy felt totally alone. A hint of fear breathed on his neck. He paced faster. Finally he knocked on the *gelateria* door. He waited and knocked again.

"Impaziente," said Graziella from behind him.

Percy spun around. Graziella laughed at him. He flushed; she had already noticed the flaw his mother often complained about—Percy was always impatient. He wished he could make a snappy comeback. Percy was good at snappy comebacks. But not in Italian.

"Mi piacciono i pantaloni," said Graziella.

Percy pulled out his dictionary and walked toward the street lamp.

Graziella pointed at his blue-striped pants. *"Sono belli."* She smiled.

Oh, yeah, she liked his pants. Okay. Good. At least he hadn't screwed that up. *"Grazie."* So now what? He opened the dictionary. Okay. *"Cosa facciamo?"* he said, which should have meant, "What shall we do?" It was lame, he knew, but it was the best he could manage.

"Vieni con me." Graziella took off across the *campo* toward the bridge to San Pantalon.

Percy followed obediently. They walked through one

alley after another, crossing bridges, always rushing. A woman skimmed past Percy in an equal hurry and their passing arms slammed hard against each other's. The shopping bag on her shoulder fell off, scattering little parcels. Percy stooped to help gather them. When he stood up again, Graziella was out of sight and Percy was alone in a dark, narrow alley. He ran to the first turnoff but Graziella was nowhere in sight. He called out softly, "Graziella." He didn't want to shout her name. That seemed rude somehow. He made his voice deeper, hoping it would carry farther. "Graziella." Nothing.

Percy took a deep breath. Okay, she couldn't be far. He went to the next turnoff. Still no one. But she must have turned here, otherwise she'd still be in sight, right? He turned and rushed along as quickly as he could without running. He got to the next turnoff. No one.

Percy Trevisan was lost in Venice in the middle of the night. He shut his eyes and leaned against a wall. The stones felt cool and damp through his T-shirt. The air reeked of someone's dinner. Everything about this place was foreign to him—the very smells were exotic. Percy opened his eyes. It didn't make much difference; the alley was dark and gloomy. Percy was lost.

Yeah. Okay. Better not to think too much about it. He walked along slowly, came to a bridge, and stopped. He leaned on the railing. He swallowed hard and faced facts:

She had abandoned him. What reason was there not to be rude? He shouted as loudly as he could, "Graziella!" His voice echoed up and down the tiny canal. A dog barked. Angry voices came from inside the window closest to the bridge. Oh, no. He'd probably woken every little kid within a square mile. He went to the center of the bridge and sat down, letting his legs hang over the edge. He crossed his ankles and waited.

"Ciao, Stracciatella." Graziella stood on the other side of the bridge.

Percy looked at her and sighed. He pulled out his dictionary and realized how pitiful an act that was on this dark night. He put his left hand over his eyes and put the dictionary back in his pocket. It was going to be a silent night. Percy, whose only strength in dealing with girls was his quick wit, wouldn't be able to say anything tonight. He slapped the ground beside him and turned his face back toward the canal.

Graziella came onto the bridge and sat beside Percy. "It is okay," she whispered. "Speak English."

Percy's heart raced. "I knew you spoke English." He almost sang, it was such a relief to be able to speak spontaneously. Now he'd be able to really talk to her. He could even joke around and just be who he really was. "I knew it, I just knew it."

"I speak very good English," said Graziella.

"Your schools must do a better job than American schools—just from those few words I can tell your English is a lot better than my Spanish."

"Spanish?"

"I take Spanish in high school."

Graziella gave a little sniff of indignation. "I did not learn in school. I took private English lessons for many years. It is important to speak the language of the oppressor. Japanese, I study now, too."

"The oppressor? You talk like we're at war."

"We are, in a way."

"Italy and the United States are at war?" Percy shook his head. "You may be smart at languages, but I think political science isn't your strong point."

"And you are perhaps as quick to arrive at wrong judgments as you are impatient."

"Yeah," said Percy, "excellent English." He smiled at her.

She didn't smile back.

Percy dropped the smile. "It must be expensive to take private lessons."

Graziella nodded. "I work. I pay for what is necessary." Her tone was belligerent.

What was the point in avoiding it? Graziella seemed to want a confrontation—and Percy had nothing else to talk about. "So explain to me how Italy and the United States are at war."

"Not Italy, Venice. And it is not a war, no, because the Venetians have not yet begun to fight back. But we prepare. We rally. We will reclaim our rights."

"I can't understand you at all," said Percy.

"But I think you can," said Graziella. "You understand the powerless."

"I do?" said Percy, feeling stupid.

"Do not act, how do you say, coy? You are big, strong American boy. Almost man. You are rich. You are beautiful. You are smart."

Beautiful? Did she say "beautiful"? Percy was too slight, too fine-featured to be considered handsome in America. But Graziella couldn't possibly have misunderstood such a common word. So she must have meant it. She thought Percy was beautiful. His cheeks went hot with pleasure. "I'd say thank you if I didn't think that in your own perverse way you had just insulted me. Anyway, you've got one thing absolutely wrong. I'm not rich."

She laughed. "But you agree you are beautiful, smart, big, and strong?"

Percy made a low whistle. "Busted."

"What?"

"It's an expression we used to use when I was a kid. It means you got me, you made a fool of me."

"You helped Matteo. You are not fool," said Graziella. "And some things, some important things, you understand them."

"Is that why you agreed to see me tonight? Just because of my liking Matteo?"

"Yes," said Graziella. "This made you interesting."

"And is that why last Sunday you gave me peach ice cream when I asked for *stracciatella*? Last Sunday, before I'd ever met Matteo?"

Graziella looked out over the canal. She whispered, "Busted."

Percy laughed.

Graziella laughed. "So we are both human, eh? We both think you are beautiful."

"You're the beautiful one."

Graziella looked at her hands. "Your beauty, it causes problem for me. It is what made me act like that last Sunday, even when I found out you were American." She got up. "Come. We will go more slowly."

"Just where are you taking me?"

"To a club."

"A nightclub? It'll be filled with those American oppressors you hate."

"Not a *stupido* nightclub. A club where only Venetians go. The real Venetians."

"Who are the real Venetians?" asked Percy.

"They are the people no one cares about, the people no one sees." Graziella moved along, gaining speed as she went.

"And the fact that no one sees them has something to

do with why Americans are the oppressors?" asked Percy in a joking tone.

Graziella stopped dead in her tracks. She took Percy's arm and pulled him to a halt. They stood in the dark alley, their bodies less than a foot apart.

"You're small." Percy leaned over her now. "Your hair smells of something woodsy."

"And you are obvious." Graziella's voice quavered a bit. Percy couldn't tell if it was from anger. He wished he could see her face better. She spoke firmly: "This is not joke. If you come with me tonight, you must not act like it is joke. You must not embarrass me. So do not talk."

"I can't talk?" Percy said in a whine.

"No."

"And if I don't agree, I suppose you'll abandon me to wander for the rest of my life among the alleys of Venice."

"You will manage," said Graziella. "Americans always do."

"The way you say it, you make me feel I should be ashamed I'm American."

"We talk about shame later. Now we hurry. Do you agree?"

"My lips are sealed."

"What?"

"It's an expression. It means I won't breathe a word. But actually you use it when you're promising someone you won't give away a secret, so it doesn't fit here. Sorry."

"It fits." Graziella lifted her braid to Percy's nose. "It is balsam, *Signor Stracciatella. Cavaliere.*" She took him by the hand and pulled him at a running speed.

Percy almost fell. He hadn't expected her hair in his nose. He hadn't expected her hand holding his. He felt like a huge dumb animal beside a clever little fox. Maybe he was an ox. Lightweight Percy Trevisan was an ox for the first time in his life. Did a bull ox feel this excited by the flick of a cow ox's tail? He wanted to catch hold of her by that silver clip on the end of her braid—he wanted to catch and pull her to him. And why had she called him *cavaliere*? Percy felt anything but cavalier.

They turned, crossed another bridge, turned. Abruptly they were ringing a bell and there was a buzz and the door in front of them opened. Graziella whispered to Percy, "Do you know about Italian dialects?"

"What's to know?" asked Percy.

"Everyone here speaks in *veneziano,* not Italian. But if anyone addresses you, since you are stranger, they will speak Italian. Just nod. I take care of you."

Percy nodded.

They climbed marble steps, passed through a hall where the plaster had fallen off in huge chunks, and entered a smoke-filled room packed with young people deep in conversation.

A guy near Percy gesticulated passionately with a cigarette between his fingers. Percy had to duck to avoid get-

110

ting burned. He whispered in Graziella's ear, "Don't they know about lung cancer?"

"Zitto!" said Graziella harshly.

Percy didn't need to translate: He shut up.

Graziella joined the fringe of a heated debate. Percy heard the word *Expo* and understood that they were all united against Expo's being in Venice. But they disagreed on something else he couldn't catch. Venetian sounded a lot like Italian. Sort of a slushy Italian. Graziella nodded vehemently several times. At one point people laughed and applauded. Percy looked around the crowded room. There was a bar in one corner. He went to buy a drink, wondering how he could do it without talking. Would Graziella care if he talked if all he was doing was buying them drinks? She might. Percy felt suddenly conspicuous. He looked down. His shoes were made in the United States. His socks. His T-shirt. His underwear and bones, for those who had X-ray eyes. Thank God Mom had bought him the striped pants. On the wall near the bar he saw the painted words AMERICANI, AMERICAGNE. Percy recognized the pun: *Cani* meant dogs; *cagne* meant bitches. A sweat bead rolled down his neck.

An arm came slapping across his shoulders. *"Salve,"* shouted Alessandro above the din.

Percy's shoulders dropped. Not only was his rival for Graziella here, but now everyone would find out he was American. He mustered the most noncommittal look he could and shouted back, *"Salve,"* which seemed to be another way to say *ciao*.

Alessandro elbowed his way through the crowd in front of Percy and led him to the bar. *"Due,"* he said to the bartender.

"Tre," corrected Percy. He didn't know what drink they were ordering, but whatever it was, they needed three.

Alessandro gave Percy an appraising look. Then he nodded to the bartender and slapped 1500 lire on the bar. *"Tre."*

The bartender filled three plastic cups with beer from the tap. Alessandro handed two to Percy and took a gulp from the third.

Percy put one beer back down on the bar and reached into his pocket for money.

"Lascia stare." Alessandro put the cup of beer back into Percy's hand and smiled a genuinely friendly smile.

"Grazie," said Percy, with a searching look.

Alessandro laughed. *"Sono il cugino di* Matteo." He backed off and made his way toward the direction he had come from.

So Alessandro was Matteo's cousin. By taking care of that one little boy Percy had broken the ice with both Graziella and Alessandro. A strange bit of luck.

A man backed into Percy and knocked beer down the

front of his shirt. *"Eh, scusa,"* he said. He looked at Percy with curiosity.

Graziella leaned around Percy's arm. "Carlo, *ti presento il mio amico Stracciatella.*"

Carlo held out a hand. Percy took it and shook. *"Piacere, Stracciatella,"* said Carlo with a smile.

Percy smiled back. Graziella had introduced him with a nickname: *Stracciatella.* It might be absurd as an Italian name, but it was infinitely better than "Percy" for this setting. It felt good. He wanted to say *piacere* to Carlo. He was sure he could say it right. But Graziella held on tight to his arm in what he knew was a warning. He nodded silently.

Carlo moved off and Graziella pulled Percy to a corner. She took a beer from him and sipped, looking at him over the top of the cup. Percy took a mouthful of beer and shut his eyes for a moment as it went down his throat. The noise was terrific; the smoke was choking; the crowd was too thick for comfort. Yes, it was a change from the last time he'd shut his eyes, alone back there in the alley twenty minutes ago. But he wasn't sure it was a welcome change. He had always been slightly claustrophobic. He wasn't panicky yet, but he could feel the tension rising. He opened his eyes, took Graziella by her free hand, and pushed through to the door.

Once out in the alley, he pulled Graziella, turning at the

first side alley and heading for a street lamp. They came out all of a sudden in Campo San Pantalon, just across the bridge from his own Campo Santa Margherita.

Percy looked around in amazement. "You led me in circles just so I wouldn't know where the club was. How come?"

Graziella drank her beer and looked out over the canal.

Percy's heart sped as the thought hit him: "Is the club illegal?"

"Not illegal," said Graziella. "Just unpopular among some people who think they are important." She finished her beer and put the cup in the trash can by the bridge.

"What's the story on Expo?" Percy crumpled his empty beer cup and tossed it overhand into the trash beside Graziella's cup.

"What do you think about tradition?"

"Tradition?" said Percy stupidly.

Graziella took a small white paper bag out of her pocket. She reached in and handed Percy a flat quarter-moon cookie. She took one herself and ate it.

Percy ate his. It was dry and mildly sweet. "Nothing to write home about."

Graziella smiled. Her dimples were deep, so deep. "These biscuits are *baicoli*. People have been making them in Venice since forever. I eat them often. Once a week. More."

"I guess the taste grows on you."

"I hate them," said Graziella. "Everyone does. But they are tradition."

Percy nodded. "My mom is in a quandary because people want her to use plastic bags for garbage. It's not the same thing as tradition, really, but it's similar. She says it's a case of when in Rome do as the Romans do."

"We have that, too: *'Paesi che vai, usanze che trovi.'* It means, 'Countries that you go, customs that you find.'"

"Sort of a shorthand way of saying it," said Percy.

"We have many proverbs about customs. Some are very ugly. The worst I think is: *'Donne e buoi dei paesi tuoi.'* It means, 'Women and oxen from your own country.' It tells a man to pick them both from where he lives. Then he knows they have the right legs to work the dirt of the country of the man."

"Wow." Percy remembered the sign on the boat the other day: MEN DON'T PROTECT YOU ANYMORE. His skin went all goose bumps. He felt accused—unfairly: Just being male didn't make him the enemy. "That proverb's not exactly feminist."

Graziella gave Percy an appraising look. "Your mother will not use plastic garbage bags. Why not?"

"The environment."

"Maybe I like your mother," said Graziella.

"I'm her son," said Percy.

Graziella smiled again.

"You have a beautiful smile," said Percy.

Graziella looked at him, as if daring him. Half the time Percy had been with her he'd felt she was daring him. Her eyes were dark. So much darker than her hair.

Percy hesitated. Then he went to the bridge steps and sat under the street lamp. "Expo?"

Graziella sat beside him. "Once there were clubs for Venetians all over town. Now there are a few *osterie* that the tourists do not yet clutter up. That is all that remains to us. We started this club a half year ago. No tourist enters."

"I feel honored," said Percy.

Graziella looked at him sharply. "Do you joke now?"

"No, I'm totally serious."

She pointed around the *campo*. "What do you see?"

Percy followed her finger. "Nothing. Closed shutters. A light here or there. Some dark windows."

"Do you close your shutters at night?"

"No," said Percy. "It's way too hot."

"Exactly. All those apartments there, the shuttered ones, all are empty."

Percy shook his head. "So what?"

"There is a housing shortage in Venice. Understand, please: There are plenty of empty homes. But these empty homes, they are owned by rich foreigners who come for a week or two a year and leave them empty the rest of the time."

"Foreigners?" Percy felt the lash of prejudice sting his face. "What about rich Italians?"

"Yes, you are right," said Graziella. "You are smart. I said that before. It is true. Venice is the victim of rich Milanesi, as well. And the homes not owned by the rich, they are in need of restoration. But the city will not allow anyone to buy them unless they promise to restore them."

Percy stood up. "If people want to live in places that need repairs, then surely they should want to make the repairs."

"Restoration is more than repairs. It does not mean making a home, how do you say, inhabitable. It means making the facade look like the original. In the sixteen hundreds. The fourteen hundreds, even. Restoration means replacing all the windows with new ones that are in the old style, windows that cost much and let in little light. It means things you, the American boy with no sense of history, would never dream—and these things, they cost money."

"Americans have a sense of history," said Percy, letting an edge creep into his voice.

"I do not think so. Americans want the newest things for themselves, but they come to Europe to find old things. As if an old building will, how do you say, reassure them that they do, after all, have a past."

Percy chewed at a hangnail on his thumb. "Americans don't tell your city what to restore."

"Not directly. The city does that itself. All so that Venice can look the same forever. But that goal is not ours—the goal is yours. Everything is to please the tourist."

"Not all tourists are American."

"No. Not all." Graziella scratched her arm vigorously. "The Japanese and Arabs mimic the Americans."

A heaviness came over Percy. The weight of responsibility. But at the same time he was angry that Venice was so weak kneed. If the city buckled under to the whims of tourists, it was Venice's fault, no one else's. "All the same," said Percy slowly, letting each word sound as rational as he could make it, "all the same, it comes down to Venice deciding for itself. Tourists don't make city policy."

"But they do. They say Venice is timeless. They don't want change. And our city council is seduced. They want to survive."

"Just a moment ago," said Percy very softly, "you ate a cookie you hate because of tradition. You don't want certain things to change."

Graziella stood and faced Percy. "Everything has changed for the Venetians. *Baicoli* are one of the few things we have left. Whatever we had that did not serve the tourists, whatever we had that did not bring revenue to the city, they took away. The only jobs now are those that service the tourists. Families have moved away because there are no services for family life: Children do not bring the city revenues."

"There's Estate Ragazzi," said Percy.

"Estate Ragazzi is run by the Salesiani priests, not by the *comune,* the city," said Graziella. "We, the *animatori,* we work because we fight for the children. We work as volunteers because children have no price tag. We work to keep hope of a future for Venice. Without the children, the city is nothing but museum." Graziella's eyes glittered with emotion.

Percy touched her lightly on the shoulder. "A museum. And maybe soon an amusement park if Expo comes to Venice." It was getting through to him. "I see."

"Do you?"

"I think so," said Percy. "At least a little."

"Should we go back to the club now?"

"No." Percy leaned over his knees and rubbed at a spot on his sneaker.

"Why not, *Signor Stracciatella*?"

Percy straightened. "I hate breathing the smoke."

Graziella's eyes grew suspicious. "You think Americans are better because they have decided smoking is sin? Americans make everything pleasurable sin."

"You know smoking is stupid. But you can't admit that about your friends." Percy cocked his head. "But you don't smoke. You don't have any bad habits. You do everything just right—at camp and at work."

"You accuse me of being perfectionist?"

"Absolutely," said Percy.

119

"Americans love mediocrity," said Graziella. "It is the inheritance—no, how do you say, the legacy, yes, it is the legacy of Protestantism."

"I don't understand."

"You work so hard to fit, to be like everyone else, that you cannot bear perfection. Americans resent achievement."

"And you deal too much in stereotypes," said Percy.

Graziella gave him a cool glance. "You do not?"

Percy folded his hands together. He wasn't used to this kind of talk. When he got together with friends back home, they joked and teased—they didn't make everything so heavy and serious. And when something truly important was on their minds, they stepped lightly, always ready to pull back if it looked as if they were about to make fools of themselves. Everyone stayed cool. But it seemed impossible to stay cool with Graziella. She saw the world differently. So if he was going to have a chance at knowing her, he had to try hard to get past the huge barriers she kept erecting. He turned to her and let the words come as openly as he could bear. "When I look at you, I see a fuzzy outline. Your words bring you into focus briefly, then the next words make you all fuzzy again. But I'm looking hard. I'm trying to see you. Not some fixed image of who you might be or should be or could be. Just you. Whoever you are."

Graziella held her mouth slightly open and looked at

Percy with sadness in her face. She glanced at her watch and bit her bottom lip. "Do you know your way home?"

"Sure. I live on Rio Nuovo across the first bridge on the other side of Campo Santa Margherita."

"Ah. Then I know where you live. The top floor, the student apartment, no?"

"Yes."

"Okay, then. I go home now, *Stracciatella*. Good night."

"I'll walk you home."

"I can go alone."

"Of course you can," said Percy. "I'd like to walk you. Will you let me?"

"You might not be able to find your way back."

"I know my way home from the prison," said Percy.

Graziella did a double take. "How do you know I live behind the prison?"

"Accident," said Percy. "I was wandering around early Monday morning and I saw you cross the bridge."

Graziella looked thoughtful. "Yes. I had to buy some things for my grandmother before I left for Estate Ragazzi on Monday. I was late. But I did not see you."

"I wanted to call to you, but I didn't know your name." Percy and Graziella were walking again, this time side by side, easily. "Why is the bridge gate locked?"

"To keep people out," said Graziella. She gave a small laugh.

"What people?" asked Percy.

"I do not even know," said Graziella. "Maybe the utility company asked for it when they first put the prison there."

"The utility company?"

"Yes. That housing area is only for public employees. Many of them work for the utility company. Some of them are police, military, things like that." Graziella's hands moved as she talked, fluttering in the night air like bats. "Maybe the utility company was worried about the men in prison."

"So only men are there?"

"The women's prison is on Giudecca."

"Are they dangerous men?"

"Dangerous enough to be locked up. Not dangerous enough to be kept miles from other people." Graziella moved ahead of Percy as they turned down a narrow alley. "Sad men more than bad men."

"More of the powerless?" asked Percy.

"Yes."

"Do you see the whole world in political terms?"

"Think of how we met," said Graziella. "Not a very political moment, I think."

Percy smiled.

They crossed the bridge together.

CHAPTER 11

The wide brim of Mom's hat stood out eight inches or more. She leaned over Christopher so that the sun passed through the red brim before it fell on his face, making him all pink.

"Come on, Mom." Percy pulled her by the arm. "The number five boat will be arriving any minute, forget the ice cream."

"But I want ice cream. Nico's *gelato* is famous. It's supposed to be the best in Venice."

"The very best is in Campo Santa Margherita," said Percy.

"That's right," said Christopher. He readjusted his backpack. He loved fiddling with it.

Mom threw her hands up in the air. "We're in Venice. I

want us to do the Venice thing. And your father wants us to do the Venice thing. This is his ancestral home. And Caterina recommends this place." Caterina was the old lace-maker who used to live on Burano—the one Mom was taking photographs of. Mom had become friends with her.

Percy tightened his hold on his mother's arm. "Easy, Mom. The boat to Murano is here, see?" He steered her to the side as the passengers got off. Christopher took Mom's other hand.

They filed on and Christopher pulled them down the steps inside the boat, past the benches, and out onto the open deck at the rear. Mom and Percy sat while Christopher got on his knees between them and leaned out over the water. They were on their way to the glass factories.

Mom clutched her hat brim. "Don't lean over so far."

"Look at the zucchini!" shouted Christopher.

Bobbing along in the water close to the *fondamenta* was a string of zucchini. There were dozens of them. A hundred. Maybe more. "Someone must have toppled a crate into the canal." Percy watched the people pass by, hardly giving a glance to the floating vegetables. Even the children were nonchalant. "This sort of thing must happen all the time," he said.

"And notice," said Mom, "no one fishes the vegetables out. The water's so dirty, no one would eat them now."

"I want to catch one," said Christopher. "We could carry it home in my backpack and clean it and fry it."

"After all," said Percy, "we grow all sorts of vegetables in shit."

"We do?" said Christopher.

"That's what fertilizer is. Or used to be, before we got into chemicals so much."

"All right," said Mom, "enough. If Venetians won't eat those zucchini, neither will we."

Percy studied his mother's profile. "Anything wrong, Mom?"

"Ducks," said Mom. "Ducks and watermelon and eggplant."

"I like watermelon," said Christopher hopefully.

Percy moved closer to his mother. "What are you talking about?"

"It's the *Festa del Redentore* tomorrow. A big celebration." Mom kept her eyes steadily on the far bank. "See that church? That's the Church of the Redentore. In the fifteen hundreds, the plague spread through this area of Italy and people died by the thousands. Two plagues, in fact—only a half century apart, I think. Anyway, the people built that church to honor God for ending one of them."

"Okay," said Percy in a reasonable tone. "So . . . what about the ducks?"

"Everyone roasts duck tonight to start the *festa*. And they also eat watermelon and eggplant. But I have no cookbooks with me here."

"We don't know what duck's supposed to taste like anyway," said Percy. "Just cook it however you want."

The boat turned down a wide canal and passed under a huge bridge. "The Arsenal's coming up," said Percy. This was one of the few sights of Venice that he'd really been looking forward to. One of Mom's guidebooks had a long section all about how Venice had ruled the seas. This city had once been one of the great economic and military powers of the world. "Look carefully, Christopher. Here's where they used to build the warships."

Christopher strained past Percy for a good look. But the Arsenal didn't seem very threatening now. Cats rambled over the weeds and stones. The sun beat down hard on piles of old iron chains and anchors. The crickets hummed in broad daylight. Christopher slumped back against Mom. Percy couldn't blame him. Why was Venice always like that—always being other than what he expected? He never felt secure about anything here.

The boat came out on the lagoon side, made its last stop in Venice, then set out across the open water for the cemetery at San Michele and then the island of Murano. Motorboats sped past, some with girls in bikinis on the bow. Did Graziella ever go in boats? Was there anything politically wrong with a bikini? Percy thought again of the sign on the boat the other day: MEN DON'T PROTECT YOU ANYMORE. It was disturbing how often he found himself thinking of that sign. No, he was pretty sure that Graziella did not own a bikini.

Dad stood by the lighthouse near the boat stop, watching for them. He waved as they docked and walked down the ramp. He had come ahead of them after an early meeting.

Mom kissed Dad on the cheek. "Vince, you take them to the glass factories. I'll see you at home later." She turned around and went back up the ramp, joining the crowd that pushed onto the boat.

Dad took Christopher's hand and looked confused. "Where are you going?"

Mom was already back on the boat. "See you later," she called, smiling and holding the brim of her hat. She took an inside seat.

"What got into her?"

"Ducks," said Christopher.

"Ducks?"

Percy shrugged his shoulders. "Don't worry about it. So how did the emergency meeting go?"

Dad scratched the back of his neck. "A wiring confusion, nothing more. We got it straight." He threw his arm around Percy's back. "They say the factories toward the center of the island are more authentic than these near the boat stop."

They walked down a side *fondamenta* and turned onto a canal that seemed toylike after Venice—small and quiet. Maybe the way Venice felt a hundred years ago. Dad turned through a gate. Two men were scrabbling around with sticks.

"A scorpion," said Christopher, stepping behind Dad and peering out around his legs.

The scorpion backed away from one man's stick and wound up climbing onto the other man's, who promptly flung it far across the dry grassy plot.

"Why didn't he kill it?" Percy asked Dad.

"Kill?" The man smiled. "Why should I kill it?" he said in good English. He rubbed his hands together. Percy felt a flush of embarrassment; the scorpion, the very idea of any scorpion, scared him. But he agreed that every creature had a right to live. The man seemed to sense Percy's discomfort. He looked at him kindly. "You came to see the furnace?"

"Sure did," said Dad. "I had a great-grandfather who worked in one of these factories as a kid. Then his family moved to Padova."

"What's your surname?"

"Trevisan."

The glassblower nodded as if he was impressed. "A good name. *Trevisan* is known throughout the Veneto." He led the way through a corridor that was dark and damp after the almost blinding sunlight outside. They emerged into a large room lit only by the glow of the fire in the huge wood-burning furnace. The blast of heat was as palpable as a blanket.

The glassblower pulled on thick gloves. He picked up a metal pipe about four feet long and dipped the end of it in the molten yellow-orange glass at the edge of the furnace. He blew and when a bulb formed, he rolled it back and forth on a marble table. Then he heated it in the furnace again and blew and shaped it with a metal pick and rolled and heated again and blew and shaped, over and over. The glass was now green with flecks of yellow; it formed a goblet. Percy thought of Katharine Hepburn in *Summertime,* the old movie Mom had checked out of the video store to get them ready for Venice. The glassblower should have used red.

Then suddenly the demonstration was over. Dad dropped money in the dish on the edge of the marble table and they walked out into the sea breeze and the bright sunlight. They walked for an hour, from display room to display room, gawking over glass crabs in smoky gray and clear sharp stallion heads and chess sets you'd never dare play with. Christopher bought a prism that had so many faces Percy didn't have the patience to count them. He tucked it away in a special inner pocket of his backpack. They ate fish soup and crusty bread; then Dad and Percy sat on the bench by the lighthouse waiting for the boat while Christopher walked in his *marcialunghe* in the shallow water at the base of the lighthouse and collected bits of broken glass in vivid colors. The edges were worn smooth from the water.

The boat that finally came wasn't the number 5, though. It was about four times larger, with an upper deck and rows and rows of seats, both indoors and out. "It'll never fit in the Venice canals," said Percy.

"This one goes through the lagoon islands and directly back to the Fondamenta Nuove at the edge of Venice without stopping," said Dad. "It never has to go through a canal. But we can easily walk from Fondamenta Nuove."

They got on and Percy raced after Christopher up the stairs to the front of the top deck. The view was stupendous. Despite the heat, the air was clear and they could see all the way to the tip of the Lido. Christopher ran around the top deck pointing at every tall tower in Venice. Percy kept his face into the wind. Tonight Percy would go to the *campo* and look for Graziella. He should have asked her last night if she could go out tonight. Oh, well. What if she wasn't working because of this *Festa del Redentore*? Percy blew through loose lips.

The boat slowed down and the loudspeaker came on. Percy made out something about an emergency stop. The boat headed toward the dock at San Michele. A very old man and woman waited to get on. Percy could see over the walls into the cemetery. People meandered around. A fat man in tan pants. And a woman with a red hat. She clutched at its wide brim. Percy turned toward Dad abruptly. "I'm getting off here."

"What?" said Dad. "This isn't a scheduled stop. They might not even let you."

"I won't ask. I'll take another boat home. See you." He ran down the stairs.

"You be home by five," Dad shouted after him. "Or six at the latest."

"Yeah," Percy shouted over his shoulder. He leapt off the boat and watched it pull away. Christopher waved to him from the top deck. Percy waved back. Christopher kept waving for as long as Percy could still make him out. So Percy waved back that long. Then he dropped his hand to his side and closed his eyes. The only noise he could hear was the water and the distant buzz of motorboats. There were no tourists crowding around at the boat stop. Maybe cemeteries were blessed places, after all.

"Percy, what are you doing here?"

Percy turned around and smiled at his mother. "I saw your hat from the boat."

"Oh." She smiled back.

"Why'd you come here?"

"I was visiting someone."

"Who?"

"Ezra Pound."

"Ezra Pound? He's buried here?"

"Mmmhmm."

"I didn't know you were such a fan of poetry, Mom."

"It's not the poetry as much as the man."

Percy's memory strained. "Wasn't he a fascist?"

Mom laughed. "Not the political man. The father, and the grandfather. I knew his grandson once."

Percy stepped back in mock shock. "My mother rubbed elbows with the high and mighty?"

"Not with Ezra Pound himself. With his grandson. He was a graduate student at Harvard. Hardly high and mighty."

"Were you in a class with him?"

"No. We were friends."

Something about the way she said it made Percy ask. "Close friends?"

Mom looked at Percy almost curiously, as though she didn't quite know him. "Yes."

"Oh." Percy looked out at the lagoon again. "I guess I never thought about your life before Dad." He looked at Mom. She was looking steadily at him. He turned back to the lagoon. "Did you love him?"

"I loved his aura."

Percy kicked at imaginary stones on the *fondamenta*. "What's that mean?"

"He was so many things I didn't understand." She hooked her arm through Percy's. "He wrote poetry in four languages."

"As good as Ezra Pound's?"

"I can't judge poetry. I just know what I like. And he sounded wonderful. I loved his accent when he spoke English."

"He wasn't American?"

"He was Italian, and a wonderful cook."

"How'd you meet him?"

Mom smiled. "Bold. I was bold, Percy. You've got to be bold some of the time."

Percy rolled his shoulders back. He looked at Mom's glowing face. He shook his head and a grin spread slowly across his face. "My mom loved an Italian."

Mom peered up at Percy. "Like mother, like son?"

Percy blushed.

CHAPTER 12

The envelope said STRACCIATELLA in block letters. Percy put the watermelon on the ground and peeled the envelope free from the gate. He ripped it open.

> *Ponte San Pantalon.*
> *Alle 8.*
> *G.*

Percy checked his watch. Seven-thirty already. He ran through the garden and took the stairs two at a time.

"Mom," he called as he ran into the kitchen.

Dad was leaning into the open oven, spooning juices over the duck and humming. "Mom's getting dressed. Going to wear something special for dinner, I guess."

"Here's the best melon I could find. There weren't many left."

Dad shut the oven. He took the melon and thumped it loudly. "Good."

Percy poured himself a glass of water, trying to think of a way to ask. Nothing brilliant came to mind. "Dad, would it be okay if I went out?"

"Out? When?"

"Tonight."

"Tonight? Tonight's the *festa*. We're going down to the Zattere to watch the fireworks at ten."

"I want to go out with a friend."

"Oh." Dad carried the watermelon to the refrigerator. He opened the door and plums spilled out and rolled across the floor. He shut the refrigerator and made his way carefully around the plums. Percy thought of an elephant tiptoeing through tulips. He smiled. Dad set the watermelon on the kitchen table and looked at the floor helplessly, as if bewildered by all these fruits. "Sure, Percy. You can have a good dinner and go."

"There isn't time for dinner."

"No time for dinner?"

"I've got to meet her at eight."

"Oh. Well, then, you better hurry."

"Thanks." Percy went to the bedroom and opened his drawer. The blue-striped pants had already been washed and sat there on top of everything. It had been a steamy day. Would he be too hot in pants? Anyway, he'd worn them last night. Okay, then, the black shorts. And the blue T-shirt. Black and blue. Like a big bruise. Not a good sign, but so what? Percy grabbed the clothes and ran for the bathroom. It took him all of seven minutes to shower, wash his hair, and shave. He slipped on his clothes and jammed the key and 30,000 lire into his pocket. He went back into the kitchen.

Christopher sat alone at the table. "You're really going out?"

"Yeah. What's wrong?"

"Mom and Dad are outside on the balcony arguing. Mom's worked hard on this meal. You knew that—you knew she was all crazy about the duck. You're dirt."

"Yeah." Percy felt a twinge of guilt. "But, look, I'm going out with Graziella."

"You are?" Christopher grinned. "That's great."

"Yeah. So help me out of this, will you?"

Christopher got up and clasped his hands together. "You want me to act like I can't breathe?"

"I don't think they'd believe you. You haven't had an attack of the croup for more than a year."

"They'll believe me." Christopher's pure little face radiated wicked delight. "They'll forget all about you."

"You'd scare them. And Dad would probably send me for a doctor, anyway." Percy shook his head. "Just take care of them for me, okay? Keep talking at dinner. And eat the duck."

Christopher made the thumbs-up sign.

Percy stuck his head out the balcony door. Mom and Dad had their arms around each other. "Night, Dad, Mom. That duck smells great. Save me some." He waved and ran out the apartment door and down the stairs before they could answer.

The *campo* was practically empty but it had an air of excitement somehow. The shutters on all the upper floors were open. Windows that had been closed the whole time Percy had been in Venice were now open and kitchen noises and family noises wafted out. People must have come to town just for the *festa*. The fruit vendors had closed up shop. The detergent store man was already locking the folding gates. And across the *campo* Graziella's *gelateria* was shuttered.

The bridge at San Pantalon was deserted. Percy checked his watch. Eight exactly. He looked around. No Graziella. He walked back to the edge of Campo Santa Margherita and looked. The *gelateria* was still shut. He went back to the bridge. By now Mom and Dad and Christopher would be sitting down to duck and eggplant and watermelon. It was eight-ten. Percy leaned over the side of the bridge.

"*Stracciatella.*"

Percy jumped and spun around.

Graziella stood there in long khaki pants with a jacket folded over her arm. She frowned at him. "Shorts? You are crazy man. On the water it is cold. We must go back to your home for other clothes."

"I can't go back home. My mother's gone nuts because I'm not eating duck with them tonight. She'd probably try to make us both stay."

Graziella smiled. "Your mother made duck? Yes, I think I do like this mother." She laughed. "Okay, come with me. They do not expect us here until nine, anyway." She took off walking fast.

Percy hurried along beside her. "Who doesn't expect us until nine?"

"My friends with the boat."

"But you said to be here at eight."

"Yes." Graziella flushed. "I thought we could use time to talk alone."

Percy nodded happily. "Alone."

Graziella speeded her steps. "Do not arrive at wrong judgment again." But her cheeks went deeper red.

Percy smiled. "Sure."

They raced along the Rio Nuovo and then past the prison, through the locked gates, and over the bridge. They went down an alley, turned into another alley, and Graziella stopped so abruptly Percy almost knocked into her. The shellac on the door in front of them was almost entirely worn off. The wood was split at the bottom in several places. Graziella opened the door with a key and pulled him into a dark vestibule. Percy felt disoriented. They were close again, in the dark again—like last night. But in an instant, Graziella was racing up the stairs.

"Isn't there a hall light?"

"Electricity costs a lot," she hissed from above.

Percy felt around and grabbed the handrail. "Even for people who work for the utility company?" He took the stairs blindly two at a time.

"We don't work for the utility company. My father was *gondoliere*—that is public servant, too. I tell you about it another time." Graziella opened the door to her apartment and they stepped into a dark room. *"Nonna?"* she called out almost in a shout.

"Tesoro, sei tu?" came an old woman's voice. The light was on in an inner room and a thin, short, white-haired woman shuffled to the doorway of the room and smiled at them. Framed in the light like that, she looked like an angel. *"Ah, un amico."*

"Il mio amico Stracciatella," Graziella said loudly. She pushed Percy toward the old woman. "This is my grandmother. Try to talk with her while I find you a jacket in my father's old things."

"How can I talk with her?" said Percy.

"Say anything. She is almost *sorda*—how do you say? She cannot hear well."

"Deaf."

139

"Deaf, yes. So speak loudly." Graziella left.

Percy smiled at Graziella's grandmother.

The old woman smiled back. Her cheeks stood out like hard apples in her otherwise loose skin. Her eyes were bright and friendly. She stepped back and gestured with her hand for Percy to enter the room.

Percy walked a few steps past her. The light came from a green-and-pink swirl of glass hanging from the center of the ceiling—handblown on the island of Murano, for sure. Her bed stood against the wall with an intricate lace spread over white sheets. The lace was undoubtedly made on Burano—maybe even by Mom's friend Caterina. A crucifix mounted above the head of the bed was alone on one wall. The other walls had paintings of gondolas on the Grand Canal and of Piazza San Marco with the Doges' Palace and of people in the costumes and masks of carnival parading through snow-covered alleys in Venice. In all the world this room could have been nowhere but Venice. Beside a round wood table on a massive carved leg was a large wood chair with arms.

"Accomodati, pure," said the old woman. She pointed at the chair.

Percy walked over and sat in the chair. And, oh, what a surprise. The seat of the chair was carved in a curve that made his body feel welcome. How could hard wood be so comfortable? He leaned back and put his hands on the arms. They were smooth and shiny from years and years of hands resting there, maybe rubbing unconsciously as the old woman watched TV. For across the room was a small TV set at a perfect angle for viewing from this chair.

A waft of wet evening air came in the only window. The lace curtain moved gently. The windowsill still glowed soft with the setting sun. The vase of flowers on the table gave off a sweet aroma.

From nowhere Percy remembered a Buddhist prayer his mother had read to him once. He'd memorized the final words because they'd drawn him so strongly: "May the whole universe be filled with peace and joy and light and love." Percy had wished that he could feel as calm and whole as those words, and now, in this room, he had an inkling that it might be possible.

The old woman shuffled to the table and rearranged the flowers. Her hands moved carefully and Percy could sense the grace she'd had as a young girl. She picked a leaf off the greens surrounding the flowers and crushed it between her thumb and forefinger. Then she held it under Percy's nose.

Percy sat up straight.

She laughed and a naughty gleam shone in her eyes. She smelled the leaf, then held it out for him again.

Percy remembered how Graziella had put her braid under his nose the night before. What strange women these were. Strange and mysterious and wonderful. He laughed and breathed in the sharp minty smell of the leaf. It made the inside of his nose prickle. He felt alive and ready.

The old woman smiled and fingered her necklace. It was a plain silver chain with a single charm hanging from it— the same silver charm that was on Graziella's hair clip.

"Eccomi," said Graziella. "Here I am." She came over and kissed her grandmother on both cheeks. *"Buona notte, Nonna,"* she said loudly.

Percy stood up. He didn't know why, but he felt compelled to touch Graziella's grandmother. *"Buona notte, Nonna."* He kissed her on both cheeks.

The old woman received his kisses as though they were the most natural thing in the world. *"Divertitevi, ragazzi."* She smiled and waved them away.

They went through the dark living room and down the dark stairs. When they were out in the alley again, Graziella handed Percy a cotton jacket. "It is all I could find. We do not have much room for storage here."

"Do you live with your grandmother?"

"Yes."

Percy wanted to ask what had happened to her parents, but he didn't want to tread where he shouldn't. "Do you keep your father's things in your room?"

"I keep them in a box above a cupboard in the kitchen."

"Oh."

"You were in my room," she added quietly.

"What? I thought that was your grandmother's bedroom."

"It was. The living room is mine. I sleep on the couch.

142

You have been everywhere in my home except the kitchen, which is tiny, and the bathroom, which is in the hall."

"In the hall?"

"We share with two other apartments."

"Oh."

Graziella gave a small *humph*. "It is not luxury like in America."

"I'm not rich, Graziella. My father is here on a job, and we've saved carefully for a long time to come this summer." Percy rolled the jacket into a tight ball. "Your grandmother is beautiful."

"What do you mean?"

"She made me think of an angel—and I don't even believe in angels."

Graziella laughed. "Yes, *Nonna* is gentle. She knows how to treat people. She understands them."

"Her room is marvelous, too. Your home is marvelous, Graziella."

"Thank you."

"What is the charm she wears around her neck? The same one that's on your hair clip."

Graziella pulled her braid over her shoulder and touched the charm. "It is *forcola*. It is the piece of wood that slides into a hole in the side of the gondola. It stands up like a fork, with only two prongs, one short and one long. It supports the oar."

"An oarlock. What a strange thing to use as a charm."

"Not so strange. Women in families of *gondolieri* wear them all the time. It is—"

"Tradition," cut in Percy.

"Yes." Graziella smiled.

They hurried to the bridge at San Pantalon.

"Graziella!" Chugging along the canal came a green wooden fruit boat all decked out for the *festa*. Four poles had been set into the wide bottom and a flat canvas roof stretched over them. From the edges of the canvas hung paper lanterns of different colors. Under the roof was a long table, like a backyard picnic table, covered with boxes and flanked with benches. Matteo sat on the floor at the front of the boat with his legs crossed Indian-style, and he wore his backpack that was just like Christopher's. Two girls and a guy sat on ledges built into the sides of the boat. And Alessandro steered the boat over to the *fondamenta*.

Percy and Graziella stepped into the boat and Alessandro pushed off, taking the rudder again. He revved the motor. Percy immediately lost his footing and fell onto the ledge nearest him. Alessandro smiled. *"Scusa."*

"Buona sera," said Percy.

Graziella snatched the jacket from Percy and threw it with hers onto a pile of jackets. Then she sat beside Percy and took his arm. She pointed to each person in turn. *"Mia cugina* Luciana."

Percy smiled and nodded. *"Piacere,* Luciana."

Luciana smiled and leaned across the table, offering her hand. Percy stood up and they shook hands. *"Piacere."*

Then he was introduced to Mara, who he thought was presented as a neighbor or a Viking, he couldn't get the Italian straight, and to the guy, Claudio. Each introduction meant a handshake and a *piacere.* When it was over, Percy watched to see if they'd all sit down now. It didn't seem to occur to them that standing in a moving boat was dangerous. But they finally agreed tacitly that they had stood long enough to be polite and everyone took a spot on the side ledges.

Percy tried to catch Matteo's eye, but the boy looked straight ahead, into the bow of the boat. He was too small to see over the top from his sitting position. Percy edged along the ledge until he was close to him. Then he scuttled like a crab over beside him. *"Ciao,* Matteo."

The boy's face lit up. *"Ciao."*

Percy didn't know what to say next. He could feel eyes on his back. What was he doing here, on this crazy boat with a bunch of strangers who spoke only Italian? Graziella was there, sure. But that wasn't enough. He wanted to be alone with Graziella—like when they walked to her home and back. All the intimacy he had felt with her then had disappeared when they'd come onto this boat. And it wouldn't come back—not tonight, at least. She'd never speak to him in English in front of these people. Percy shut his eyes and sighed. This evening wasn't going to be anything like he had hoped.

Matteo put his arms around Percy's neck and kissed his cheek lightly.

Percy opened his eyes and smiled. He straightened the straps of Matteo's backpack. Then he took the boy's hand and they went and sat on the ledge.

Alessandro steered the boat up to the first turning point. They went right, down the Rio Nuovo. Percy couldn't help admiring Alessandro's skill. The boat was heavy, much heavier than a gondola. Yet Alessandro made it turn the corner smoothly. Alessandro looked at Percy and the admiration on Percy's face must have registered on him, because he smiled proudly. *"Vuoi provare?* Do you want to try?"

Percy looked at Graziella, who studied him with an amused expression. He felt sudden resentment. Was the whole evening going to be a series of challenges? *"No, grazie."* Matteo squeezed his hand. Percy didn't dare look down at the boy's face, this boy who seemed to understand him.

Their canal emptied into the Grand Canal. A small flotilla of gondolas passed by, the center one hosting an old man playing an accordion and an even older one standing and singing "O Sole Mio." The gondolas were filled with Japanese tourists.

"Sei a ciascuna," said Alessandro. Under his breath he said to Percy, "Six in each boat, the maximum allowed by law. The Japanese always get their money's worth."

Percy nodded. Then he felt like a traitor. So the Japanese got their money's worth, so what? He could appreciate that. Americans didn't like to waste money either. If four paid the same price as six, why shouldn't they make groups of six? He looked around the boat. Maybe he should find another spot to sit, farther away from Alessandro. But Claudio had his arm around Mara and they were caught in what looked like a private conversation. And Luciana and Graziella were having some sort of animated discussion. Besides, Matteo was clinging to Percy.

Okay. So he'd sit here. But he wouldn't look at Alessandro. He leaned backward and the rim of the boat hit him hard across his shoulder blades. He leaned forward again.

They passed under the Accademia Bridge and happy tourists waved at them. Then they rounded the bend past the church of Santa Maria della Salute and came out onto the Canale di Giudecca. The huge canal was filled with boats. Families sat around tables just like the table in their own boat, already eating cold pasta salads and munching on duck. Alessandro cut the motor and dropped anchor. Graziella and Luciana went into action: They opened the boxes on the table, spread a tablecloth, set dishes, silverware, salt and pepper shakers. Percy watched in amazement. Graziella produced several boughs of oleander and arranged them at the corners of the table. She smiled over her shoulder at Percy.

Percy stood up, feeling clumsy. "Can I help?"

Graziella handed him a bowl of cold eggplant, cut into finger-sized sticks. *"Dai a tutti."* She pointed.

Percy plopped eggplant onto every plate. It smelled of garlic and lemon. He wanted to sneak a piece, but he didn't know how Italians felt about that sort of thing. Matteo stood by his side and moved with him. Percy took a stick of eggplant and offered it to Matteo. The boy ate it and smiled. Then he took a stick and offered it to Percy. Who said this kid wasn't smart? Percy let the heavenly taste rest in his mouth for as long as he could before he swallowed it down. Had Graziella made it? He looked at her.

She was watching him with a smile. *"Ti piace?"*

Did Percy like it? Is a frog's ass watertight? What word of wonder could he say? He stabbed at it. *"Fabulo!"*

Graziella laughed. *"Hai la bocca di Dante. Favoloso!"*

"What does that mean," he whispered, "that I have the mouth of Dante?"

"Fabulo," she whispered back, "that is how the word was said seven hundred years ago, in Dante's time. Today we say *favoloso.*"

"Favoloso," Percy said with feeling.

She came closer, speared another stick of eggplant on a fork, and fed Percy.

"Terrifico," he said.

She jumped back in mock offense. *"Spero di no."* Then she laughed at his bewildered face. *"Non si dice, se non fa paura."*

Percy shook his head. *"Non capisco.* I don't understand."

"Terrifico is for fear. Do you fear my eggplant?"

"No. Your eggplant is like a dream. A fantasy."

"Una fantasia? Grazie." Pleasure glowed in her face. "You are kindly welcome to the food," she said, no longer in a whisper.

The ice was broken now; Percy could speak English. Apparently this boatload of people wasn't a subset of the fanatic politicos at the club last night. Percy felt empowered. "What's that?" He pointed behind Graziella.

"The boat bridge," said Alessandro, tapping Percy on the shoulder and handing him a beer from a cooler sticking out from under the table. A series of flat pontoon boats, maybe a dozen or more, ran in a string across the canal from the Zattere to the island of Giudecca. From one boat to the next extended a plank bridge at least fifteen feet wide, with wooden railings on the sides. "Those are navy boats. People can walk across the bridge from Venice to the Chiesa del Redentore. It's the only time all year that you can cross this canal on foot. After the fireworks, crowds will make the march. Matteo came with us just so we could walk across the bridge. Tomorrow morning the people who go to mass at the Redentore will use the bridge. And by afternoon, they will take it down."

Percy took a swig of the cold beer and stifled a shiver. The wind off the water chilled. Thank heavens Graziella had lent him her father's jacket. He went over to the pile of jackets, picked it out, and slipped it on. It was way too roomy for him—but it broke the wind.

"Mangiamo." Mara opened her hands in a sweeping gesture at the table, where the plates were now filled with hot duck and *ravioli* beside the eggplant. "I hope you do not mind," she said in halting English, "the pasta comes with the main food to make more simple."

"Mind? How could I mind sitting down to a beautiful meal like this?" Percy took his seat eagerly, flanked by Mara and Matteo.

"Buon appetito," said Alessandro.

"Buon appetito," echoed around the table.

Percy took a bite of duck. It was pungent with juice and spices. He picked a rosemary needle from his tongue. "Delicious," he murmured. "How did you keep the food hot?"

"In Italy we have aluminum foil," said Mara, with a twinkle in her eye. "Perhaps America will develop someday, too."

Everyone laughed.

Percy laughed, too.

"But your mother probably would not approve," said Graziella, who sat across from Percy.

"No," said Percy, "she doesn't use it."

"We have been seduced," said Graziella. "The Americans gave the world plastic and aluminum foil. We strangle ourselves with it, while they have ecology movements."

Percy stared at his plate. He carefully moved the food so that no one kind of food touched another. Graziella's voice held a level tone, but he could feel the stridency in her words. His neck felt thick and tight. "How much is the public responsible for its industry?"

"The public buys," said Graziella.

"I bought the aluminum foil," said Mara softly. "It was on the shelf. I knew it was a trouble. But I wanted, how do you say, *la convenienza*?"

"The convenience," said Percy.

"It should not have been on the shelf," said Graziella.

"You want a strong central government," said Percy. He shook his head. "A Big Brother. That has its own problems."

Graziella got up and flipped a switch on a large square battery box. The lanterns lit up, casting a ghostly glimmer over the boat. "A responsible government," she said, sitting back down.

"A phantom," said Claudio, "a phantom who would care about the people's problems—our problems."

"Who would make it possible to marry," said Mara.

"Marry?" Percy shook his head. "What are you talking about? People can marry in Italy."

"Not in Venice," said Alessandro. "No one ordinary can afford an apartment—and if you live with relatives, crowded like fish in a can, your husband or wife cannot move into your parents' home."

"So many relatives," said Mara softly.

Percy looked quickly at Mara, then at Claudio. How long would they have to wait to marry?

"Expo will make it worse," said Claudio, and he broke into Venetian.

Alessandro cut in with words just as rapid. And suddenly they were all talking, arguing, even Luciana. Percy caught bits and pieces, but only because Graziella repeated what people said now and then. It seemed the Comune di Venezia, the town council, had voted to host Expo after all. Now it was up to some commission or other to decide whether or not to take Venice's offer. It would all be settled within two weeks. The issue now, as far as Percy could understand, was sabotage. How could they sabotage the offer so that the commission would turn Venice down?

The amazing thing to Percy was that while they argued, they ate, and with gusto. It was as though the discussion, no matter how disturbing, whetted their appetites. And now they seemed to be evaluating methods of sabotage. Percy strained to follow the conversation. He rubbed the goose bumps on his legs. Then he turned to his *ravioli* and ate, surprised at its contents. Instead of ground meat or *ricotta* cheese, he found a creamy sauce with some sort of delicatessen meat. Maybe *mortadella*. And a dark green vegetable. Spinach?

Suddenly everything was bright and there was a loud crack.

"I fuochi!" shouted Matteo. He grabbed Percy's arm and pointed. *"Guarda, guarda!"*

The sky above the basin of San Marco filled with color after color, each shape larger and more stupendous than the one before. Showers of yellow burst into pink strings and spiraled their way to the water. Green rockets shot fifty feet up, seventy-five, maybe even a hundred, and exploded into shimmering red that flowed with the grace of a willow tree. And in the background loomed the basilica of San Marco and the pink Doges' Palace. Percy looked down at Matteo's face and thought of the poem by Sara Teasdale that they'd studied in English that year: "And children's faces looking up holding wonder like a cup." He'd never really liked Teasdale before, but her poem perfectly described this moment. Maybe he should try reading her again.

He looked across the table at Graziella. She caught him looking and looked back with a troubled face. Nothing was going right between them. Graziella's face was unreadable, but Percy had the awful feeling that she was disgusted with him. No one on this boat seemed to see him as anything but a representative of America. No one but Matteo.

The fireworks went on for close to an hour. It put Fourth of July celebrations to shame. How much could Venice have spent on those fireworks? Were they for the Venetians, or the tourists? What wasn't the city doing for the people because it had spent this money on fireworks instead? But he already knew—the city wasn't dredging the canals and it wasn't paying for the restoration of the buildings and, oh, so many other things, there had to be so many other things. And here I am, thought Percy, weighing things like Graziella. Like a fanatic politico. But this isn't my city. It isn't my problem. He wanted to take Graziella aside and whisper in her ear, "It isn't my problem. Don't look to me for anything." He wanted to lure her into the mood of the *festa*. He wanted to kiss her with fireworks going off in the background. He wanted her to kiss him back. Instead, he watched the sky till the fireworks died away.

"Ora," said Matteo. *"Ora,* Alessandro."

"Va bene." Alessandro pulled up the anchor and they went over to the Zattere.

Matteo took off his backpack, pulled out a jacket, zipped it on, and slipped back on the backpack—all quickly and expertly and intently. It was clear nothing was going to stop him from going with Alessandro across the boat bridge now.

Percy suddenly got up. "Can I take Matteo across the bridge?"

Alessandro looked surprised. "He lives on Giudecca. I must take him home after we cross the bridge."

"Does he know the way?" asked Percy.

"Yes."

"Then I'll walk him home."

Alessandro smiled. "You are patient."

Patient. Percy didn't think anyone had ever called him patient in his whole life. He didn't think of it as patience with Matteo—he simply liked the boy. A lot. But it wasn't worth trying to explain that now. He smiled back at Alessandro; then he turned to the others still sitting at the table. "And thank you, *grazie,* for a wonderful meal and an interesting evening."

Everyone murmured words of goodbye. Graziella busied herself with clearing the table. She looked up at Percy only after he was already on the Zattere *fondamenta,* with Matteo beside him. But then she quickly looked down again.

"I'll return the jacket on Monday at camp," called Percy.

Graziella gave no sign of having heard him.

Percy took Matteo by the hand and they pressed their way through the crowd toward the bridge of boats.

CHAPTER 13

Percy stood before the closed door. Matteo was safely delivered back to his family. From the front of the building it was impossible to see any lights in Matteo's apartment. The boy would be asleep in moments, maybe dreaming of brilliantly colored fires in the sky. That's what he had called them: *fuochi*.

Percy could sure use a fire. It wasn't as cold on land as it had been in the boat, but it was still chilly. He'd be better off if he moved fast. He had never been on the island of Giudecca before, but he knew there was boat service. Still, he didn't feel like taking a boat home. He needed to wander.

He walked across the steel bridge that connected the separate little island where Matteo's family lived to the heart of Giudecca. He stayed on the main *fondamenta* until he was back at the Chiesa del Redentore. The area in front of the church had a carnival atmosphere. Men sold Mylar balloons and candied almonds. People pushed into the church while others pushed out.

By staying near the water, Percy managed to thread his way through the crowd and across the bridge of boats again. Then he went along the Zattere and turned into the first narrow alley. It was pitch black and the walls, only a foot away on either side, smelled sweet and wet. The alley was longer than most, maybe seventy-five feet. Percy held his hands out in front of him as he walked. He felt blind. Like when he used to shut his eyes with Anthony More on the bus after school. But then he had held his eyes closed by choice—knowing full well that if he wanted to, he could open them and sight would be his. Now he held his eyes wide open, but he could see nothing. Sight was not within his control. It was even darker here than when he'd followed Graziella up the staircase to her home. A sudden fear clutched his chest and he stumbled.

The alley opened out onto a small, surprisingly well-lit canal with a wooden bridge. On the left another ten feet away a wider canal came into the small one. Percy stood on the bridge and let his heartbeat return to normal. The water shimmered under the light. If there were any place on earth more beautiful than this, how could anyone bear it?

Percy walked slowly now. He passed a party in a garden courtyard. The people wore familiar-looking dressy party clothes. It could have been a party in Falmouth, Massachusetts.

But this wasn't Massachusetts. Percy looked up and down the building walls along the canal. There were no messages spray-painted on walls, nothing to disturb the air of peace. All the same, he felt a rush of cold down his chest.

He turned into an empty alley and ran. He came out onto a path he recognized. This was the path he'd walked a dozen times between the Accademia Bridge and his own *campo*. He turned left and forced himself to slow to a walk past the few stray couples still returning home from the fireworks. His footsteps resounded in the night quiet. His eyes scanned every wall. Outside the movie theater someone had sprayed EXPO MAI in what looked like a fresh message. So *no* had given way to *mai,* which meant "never." Sentiment was stronger in the wake of the comune's decision to offer the city up for Expo. Maybe lovers who feared they could never afford to get married had painted this wall. Percy stared at the words. They were like a slap in the face. He had nothing to do with Expo, yet he felt the words shouted at him. Percy, the American, the tourist.

Percy wanted to run again. He passed the big bookstore, where they sold texts in Italian, French, German, but nothing in English. Absolutely nothing in English, the clerk had said when he'd stopped there a few days ago. Then the fancy mask store. Venice was full of mask stores. The ones in the window here were the classic ones of carnival time, in February, when everyone put on costumes and danced in the streets. He thought of the painting on Graziella's grandmother's wall. The masks in that painting looked as if they were made of leather. But these masks in the window were chalk white with sequins and feathers and gaudy materials attached here and there. On the shelves inside, Percy could see others with long birds' beaks and wrinkled cheeks. There were a fox and a butterfly. And masks of animals Percy couldn't recognize. The carnival was a Catholic celebration, and Percy wasn't Catholic. He spoke English and he wasn't Catholic. It seemed there was nothing about Percy that was anything like Italians—anything like Graziella.

He crossed in front of the Chiesa di San Barnaba, the one he'd overheard some tourists argue about. One of them claimed this was the church in the film *Indiana Jones and the Last Crusade*—the other one was sure it wasn't. He went over the bridge, turned the corner at the supermarket, and came out on his own Campo Santa Margherita.

The *campo* was dimly lit, like a space in a dream. The constant running of water in the drinking fountain lulled him. A song to no one. Beyond the fountain the iron bars over the closed bank seemed silly. A show of muscles to a nonexistent enemy. Percy slowed his walk and rambled now, toward the fountain. He stopped. On the ground lay the crushed gray body of a baby bird. Percy squatted and nudged it with a fingertip. Then he got up and picked a leaf off the tree. He wrapped the bird in the leaf and dropped it in the garbage can. He thought of how he had dropped in the hypodermic that Christopher had found just a couple of days before.

"I made mess of things."

Percy whirled around.

Graziella sat on the bench under the tree. "I did not intend to, *Stracciatella*."

Percy let out a long breath of relief. She hadn't simply gone out of his life just like that. Still, his eyes felt heavy. "You know," he said, backing up, "not much makes sense to me tonight. I'm not sure whether I want to kick things or cry." He walked around the fountain a couple of times. He stopped on the far side of it. "I'm not the one to shake the hate out of you. I'm confused by you and I like your dimples, but I'm not up to this."

She stood up, her face hidden in the tree's shadow. *"Le mie fossette?* You like my dimples."

"I'm American. I didn't invent aluminum foil. But I'm American."

"Is there anything else you like?"

"It's prejudice. Even if statistics are on your side, it's still prejudice when you bring it down to the personal level.

Like being afraid of a black teenage boy on a subway in Boston." He hesitated. Then he remembered his mother's word: *bold*. "And I like your braid."

Graziella stepped out from the tree's shadow. She came to the fountain and held her hands under the water. "What else do you like?"

Percy made a fist of his right hand and slapped it repeatedly into the palm of his left hand. "If it were my city, I'd be ready to fight to save it, too. And maybe fighting takes anger. But there's got to be a way to win without prejudice and violence." He dropped his hands by his sides. "You need good humor. Or just plain humor. And I like your legs."

The light came from behind and made a hazy red around the wisps of her hair. Graziella flattened her hands and aimed. Water sprayed Percy in the face. "What else do you like?"

"Persuasion." Percy wiped his face on the sleeve of his jacket. The water was cold. His neck hairs stood up. "You need to persuade them that it wouldn't work, that it wouldn't be in anyone's best interests to host Expo here. Go armed with facts. And I like your smile."

Graziella took a few steps and came halfway around the fountain. "What else?"

Percy's breath came with difficulty now. "How small you are, and tight with energy."

She came the rest of the way and stood directly in front

of him. Her face was persimmon sweet. Percy shut his eyes for a second and her face stayed just as vivid before his blind eyes. He opened them. Her perfume was maddeningly faint. Her lips parted. "And?"

Percy ran his fingers down the side of her face, across her cheek, across her lips. "Your persistence."

She whispered, "Are you afraid?"

"How should I know?" Percy shook his head. "I don't think so, though."

"I am afraid."

Percy swallowed. "Of me?"

"Of who you are, what you represent."

"I'm just me, Graziella. I'm a boy. A single, isolated, very-cold-right-now boy. You can understand that if you let yourself."

"Six years past, my father and mother transferred to Padova. My father was *gondoliere,* I told you."

"Not a smart move," said Percy. "What's a *gondoliere* do in Padova?"

She smiled. "I like your stupid humor."

"And what else do you like?"

Graziella laughed. "Busted. You busted me, no?" She sucked her lower lip under her top teeth. "He had a disease. Gout. It is common for the *gondolieri.* They work all day on their feet; they strain backs and arms and thighs. Always on the water in the damp air. Most work with pain for years, until they go in *pensione.* Retirement. My father could not. He came home from work and dropped in a chair and his muscles, they got hard, like ice, frozen. He could not get up again. He often sleep, slept, in the chair. And his knees, they swell up like melon."

"There's no medication for it?"

"He tried many drugs. Anyway, they gave him early *pensione* and he transferred to Padova. There he does not face another tourist. He makes wood boat models for children."

"Do you have brothers or sisters?"

"No."

"Your mother?"

"She does many things." Graziella put her fingertips to her lips. Then she smiled. "She cooks excellently."

"So when did you move back to Venice?"

"I never left Venice. My grandmother could not live alone and she refused to move. I was always close to her. And I love it here. You are americano. I am veneziana. I do not want to leave."

Percy thought of how he'd felt, sitting in the chair in her grandmother's bedroom. "I can understand that."

"I will become no one when I have to leave."

"Why would you have to leave?"

"It is bad to talk about—I get depressed." Graziella shrugged. "And maybe I do not leave ever. My father made a *patto,* an agreement, with the city. Every *gondoliere's* license passes to his son. But my father had only me.

So the city agreed that if I stay here and marry, my husband, if he wants, can go to *gondoliere* school and inherit my father's license."

"It stays in the family." Percy touched the spot on Graziella's right cheek where the dimple appeared when she smiled. "A strange thing to inherit."

"My grandfather was *gondoliere*. My great-grandfather. As far back as I know. They all had the same post, the highest spot in all Venice, at Rialto."

Percy remembered the first time he'd gone to the day camp with Christopher and Christopher had said the Scalzi Bridge was the highest point. But Percy had guessed the Rialto, and he was right. He'd have to tell Christopher. Later.

He took Graziella's hand and looked away. He tried to make his words come out soft, ordinary, as if they were a simple remark. "Alessandro maneuvers the fruit boat very well."

Graziella's hand tightened around his. "Alessandro wants to be *gondoliere*. We know each other, have known each other, from birth. We grew up together. Like brother and sister." She hesitated. "Brother does not marry sister."

Percy wove his fingers between Graziella's. "Every boy in Venice must dream of becoming a *gondoliere*."

"There are few boys in Venice." Graziella pulled her hand free of Percy's and crossed her arms at her chest. "Our population was almost two hundred thousand when

164

my mother was my age. Now it is less than seventy thousand. By the end of the century it will be under sixty thousand, and most of that will be the old or the wealthy. Every boy in Venice has two dreams. One dream is to become *gondoliere*. The other is to escape Venice."

"Escape," said Percy softly.

"It is good to be proud of oneself. No one dreams of being slave to the tourists."

They were under the light now. Percy stopped and faced Graziella. "And you dream of a Venice people will want to stay in, raise a family in."

"I have many dreams."

Percy touched Graziella's arms. She let her hands fall to her sides. He did the same. "If you had a *gondoliere* husband, you'd hassle him for working for the tourists."

"Probably."

"But you'd be proud of him for carrying on the tradition."

She smiled. "Probably."

"Graziella . . ."

She moved toward him. "*Dimmi,* speak up, *Stracciatella.*"

"I'd like . . . Could I . . ." Percy gave a half laugh. "The words won't come."

"I wait and listen."

Percy looked around, as though the *campo* itself would offer him help. The little bar beside the egg man's shop had boxes of candy in the window with ribbons tied in huge bows at one corner of each box. "We have Italian candies in the States. Baci. They're wrapped in blue and silver foil and they come with little sayings."

"I know them," said Graziella.

"All the sayings have the word for 'kiss' in them."

Graziella laughed. "The American version. In Italy we have sayings in them, too. But the sayings, they are about love, not just kiss, kisses."

"Oh." Percy couldn't think what to say next.

"Do you like them?" asked Graziella.

"Yes."

"The next time you order *gelato,* I will give you a cone of *gianduia.* It tastes like the candy."

"Oh."

"Is that all you have to say?"

"No."

Graziella swallowed. Percy watched her throat move. *"Dimmi,"* she whispered. "Tell me."

Percy's mouth went dry.

Graziella stood on tiptoe and kissed him on the lips.

Percy reached for her.

She backed off, taking his hand. "In the back of the *gelateria,* we have an office. There is a sofa. Old and uncomfortable."

"I've never heard of anything better in my whole life."

CHAPTER 14

"Just where do you think you're going?" Dad held his pen poised over the planning sheet on the table. Mom sat on the couch and watched, her eyes going back and forth between Dad and Percy.

Percy stood with one hand on the doorknob and the door already half-open. "I'll be home early."

"What's that mean, early tomorrow morning?"

Percy put his lips together and let his mouth fill with air. As he slowly let the air out, he tapped his fingers against his lips. He made a puttering sound, like a motor that couldn't get started. "I told you I was sorry about last night."

"This morning," said Dad, "not last night."

"Dad, I'm seventeen."

Mom looked down and spoke into her lap. "And you're

in a foreign country and you don't speak the language and anything could have happened to you and—"

"It's okay." Dad put his hand up toward Mom. "I'm handling it. We've already been through all that." He turned back to Percy.

"You're the one who encourages adventure, Mom."

Dad cleared his throat. "Where are you going?"

"To this place," said Percy.

"What place?"

"It's a place. Where young people get together. A place."

"A discotheque?" asked Dad.

"They talk, that's all. No dancing. No loud music."

Dad nodded. "Teenagers talk?"

Percy shrugged his shoulders. "You going to start insulting me now?"

"I didn't mean to insult. I just want to know what's going on."

"It's sort of a political meeting."

"Political?" Mom leaned forward.

"Communist?" asked Dad. "I thought the communist party had all but died. It's not led by kids from Udine, is it? Udine isn't that far away."

"What's Udine?"

"The center for neofascism in Italy today." Dad shook his head. "I don't want you around those neofascists."

"I don't know what it is, Dad, but it's not neofascist,"

said Percy. "It's sort of social activism. They don't talk about philosophy. They talk about specific problems."

"Like what?" Dad sat down. "Tell me about it."

"I'll be late."

"Better late than never."

Percy shut the door and walked over to the table. He sat down opposite Dad. "They're opposed to having Expo here."

"So am I," said Mom.

"Anyone in their right mind is," said Dad.

Percy got up. "All right, then."

"Just one minute, young man." Dad tapped his pen on the paper plans. "What time will you be home? What time exactly?"

"Before midnight, okay?"

"And if you're late, you'll call," said Mom.

"I won't be late." Percy walked to the couch and kissed his mother's cheek. "I promise." Then he whispered, "Adventure."

She closed her lips and sucked them in. But she nodded.

Percy left.

The night was cooler than Saturday night. It was downright cold. But Percy had come prepared this time: He had on a jean jacket and long pants. The surface of the water in the Rio Nuovo formed little peaks that glistened under the streetlight. Percy turned his small collar up against the wind and hurried to the *campo*. The *gelateria* was empty but for Graziella.

"Ciao, amore." He went behind the counter and took Graziella into his arms.

"Abbiamo un pubblico," she said, pulling back. "We have a public."

Percy looked around. "I don't see anyone watching."

Graziella looked around carefully. "Okay." She gave him a soft kiss. "You call me *amore,* 'love.' You are romantic."

"Sloppy romanticism." Percy tightened his hold on her. "That's exactly how I feel."

"Tonight," she said, freeing herself and running a cloth over the surface of the counter, "we work. There is much to do."

"I have to be home by midnight."

Graziella smiled. *"Mia nonna,* my grandmother, she sleeps like *ghiro,* how do you say?"

"I don't know. What's *ghiro*?"

"A little furry animal." Graziella went past Percy into the storeroom. She came back with an open dictionary even more worn than Percy's. "A dormouse."

"What's a dormouse?" said Percy.

Graziella shrugged. "It is what we say when someone sleeps so hard they do not wake at ordinary sounds." Graziella put the dictionary back on the shelf. "It is because she is near deaf."

"Okay. Your grandmother sleeps like a log."

"A log? Part of a tree?"

"That's it." Percy laughed. "We're more imaginative than you, obviously. We think of wood as sleeping."

Graziella pushed Percy playfully in the stomach. "My grandmother sleeps like a log and I can return at any hour. Your parents woke?"

"They were up waiting."

"Ahi!" Graziella yelped. "That is bad." She pulled Percy by the hand, going from one switch to another, shutting off the lights. When they were all out, Percy kissed her for a long time. Then they went outside and closed and locked the shutters.

They walked quickly, without speaking, over to Campo San Pantalon and along a small alley to the club. Even from the door on the alley, Percy could hear noise up above. The club must be jammed. And as they went up the stairs, he saw he was right. People crowded out into the stairwell. A man stood on a chair and lectured, turning around to face each part of the room in succession. He held his left hand in the air with the thumb and index finger extended. With his right hand he pointed at the crowd and spoke with vehemence and power. Suddenly the crowd broke into applause. The man put up a third finger on his left hand and tapped it insistently with his right index finger.

Percy whispered close to Graziella's ear. "What's he counting off?"

"Options," she whispered back.

Options for what? he wanted to ask. But the crowd was too close for comfort. He didn't want to cause Graziella, or himself, any problems with his English. He listened hard. He picked up words about San Marco. Maybe tables in the piazza. Maybe something about a bar. The Florian, the famous bar right there in the Piazza San Marco. Why would they be talking about a bar? Percy looked around the room. No one was scruffy. Not like a group of lefty students in America. They had clean faces and spiffy-looking clothes. But the intensity and earnestness in their eyes marked them as politicos. None of them belonged at the Florian.

Now they were cheering again. The man held up a fourth finger, which he squeezed with his right hand and shook out in front of him as if he were trying to squelch the life out of it. He talked about *gondole* now. And a *sciopero*. Percy knew that word—anyone who stayed in Italy for more than a week knew that word: strike. The *gondolieri* might strike? How ridiculous. Whom would they strike against? Their money came from the tourists, not from some centralized boss. At least, their ordinary daily money came from the tourists. But they were, after all, state employees. Percy knew that from Graziella. And when he'd talked to Dad about it this morning, he'd found out all transportation workers in Italy were state employees.

Cigarette smoke billowed out into the stairwell. A woman close by lit up. Percy made his way over to the window and leaned out. The back of the building opened directly onto a tiny canal. The wind whistled between the buildings, and the water in the canal moved along as though alive, an undulating sea creature. A woman stared at him from her window across the canal.

The woman had gray streaks in her pinned-back hair, an expensive beauty salon look. Her face was well lit from inside the apartment and Percy could see her red lipstick and heavy eyeliner. She leaned on the window ledge with her forearms, hands folded, fingers laced together. She wore a white blouse with what looked like hand-sewn lace. Maybe Burano lace again—the people here supported their own industries with a passion. The edges of the collar ruffled in the wind. The woman stood up suddenly and gave Percy a look of utter hatred. From inside she released the sliding, slatted shutter. It clattered to a close.

Percy felt queasy. What had he done to earn such open hostility? Could she tell just from looking at him that he was American? He turned his back on the window and searched the crowd for Graziella. She looked over at that moment and met his eyes with warmth and friendship.

That was when the siren sounded. It seemed to be almost directly outside. People pushed toward the door. The man on the chair shouted orders. Now everyone shouted.

Percy was pressed against the window ledge. It was too high for him to get pushed out, but he felt panicky.

There was a tremendous noise at the bottom of the stairs. From a boat out in the canal boomed a voice through a megaphone. Curses of *maledetti poliziotti,* "damned police," surrounded Percy. He shouted, "Graziella! Graziella!"

People pushed down the stairs and police pushed up, grabbing people at random. Percy edged his way backward into the corner of the stairwell. A policeman went past and grabbed the man who had lectured from the chair. He jammed the man's face against the wall and handcuffed him from behind. A woman jumped on the policeman. He swung his arm and knocked her to the ground. Percy moved toward her instinctively. Another policeman caught him by the arm and shoved him against the wall. Percy's cheekbone slammed against the plaster.

"I'm not fighting," he shouted. "You don't have to slam me. I'm not resisting."

The policeman yanked Percy around to face him. "Americano?"

"Yes. Of course," Percy said loudly.

"Go," shouted the policeman. He waved Percy away. "Go now!"

"Not without Gra . . . Grace." Percy looked around. Graziella struggled against a policeman who was trying to handcuff a young man. "Grace!" Percy shouted. "Come on!" He forced his way over and took her by the arm. "Come on, Grace, we're going home." Graziella looked at him, her mouth open. Her chin was scraped raw and bleeding. "Home to the Danieli," he said loudly. She shook her head. "Not another word," he half-shouted. "Mom's waiting for us." Her eyes flashed sudden comprehension and she nodded, taking Percy's hand. They went down the stairs and Percy said loudly the whole way, "Excuse us, watch out, we're coming through, look out, excuse us."

They moved quickly through the dark alleys and didn't stop or talk until they were safely in Campo Santa Margherita. Percy went to the fountain and washed Graziella's chin. She wet her hand and ran it across Percy's cheekbone. The wet stung. "We both are injured," said Graziella.

"What was that all about?"

"You should not have taken me away." A look of realization crossed Graziella's face as her own words sank in. "I should not have gone with you." She stepped away from Percy. "It is better to be arrested. It is better to protest hard and loud."

"Have you ever been arrested?" Percy asked.

"No."

"Well, you don't want to be."

Graziella's eyes narrowed. "Have you been arrested?"

"No."

She put her hands on her hips. "Then what do you know about it?"

"Americans have a better imagination, we already decided that, remember?"

"*Che sacco di balle.* What a lot of bull. You make jokes at wrong times."

"You think you'd have been better off in jail?" Percy's voice rose. "How effective could you be from a jail cell?"

Graziella chewed at her bottom lip.

"Anyway, you didn't get arrested." Percy hesitated, then he decided to risk it. "And you didn't get arrested because they thought—" A slow smile crossed his face and he let his tone tease. "Get this, they thought you were American."

Graziella's eyes stayed a moment on Percy's smile. The edges of her mouth twitched.

"A rich American," said Percy.

"The Danieli, *o dio mio,* the Danieli." Graziella laughed. "Imagine me in the Danieli with all the wealthy tourists. You are crazy person."

"A very rich American." Percy stepped toward her and put his index finger on the top of her head. Then he ran it slowly down the center of her forehead, down her nose, her lips, her scraped chin, her neck, down between her breasts. He stopped at her waist. "Yup," he said with a grin, "an American who stays at the Danieli. The very best hotel in all of Venice. Five stars on a four-star rating. Tapestries on the walls. Chandeliers. Silk wallpaper. Snails from room service. Satin slippers."

"You sound like you have been in it."

"Never!" Percy lifted his chin high. "I am American to the core. I imagine it."

Graziella took Percy's hand in both of hers and held it tight. "Maybe you will teach me humor."

"I'm giving it my best shot." Percy closed his other hand around Graziella's. "Tell me what that meeting was about."

"Domenico, the one speaking, he gives our strategy for the next week."

"Strategy to sabotage Expo?"

"*Esatto!* Exactly."

"What was that bit about the Florian bar?"

"There will be holdup there."

"A holdup." Percy's mind went numb. "A holdup. You mean a robbery with a gun?"

Graziella licked her lips. "You are upset."

"I'm not a thief. I didn't know you were."

She snorted. "Venice is supposed to be the safest city in all Europe. It is promoted that way. The tourists want it that way. We have no crimes. Have you noticed? We hardly have beggars. The police take them away immediately. They are unseen. Like all the true veneziani."

"So you will bring crime to Venice?" Percy shook his head. "That's stupid, Graziella."

"It is not stupid." She jerked backward, as though he had been holding her and she was freeing herself. But Percy hadn't been holding her. His hands had released hers at the word *holdup*. Graziella opened her palms and looked at them a moment. Then she closed them into fists. She held her fists in front of her chest. "It is not stupid, no."

"Yes it is. Will there really be a gun?"

"Of course."

"Then it's truly the dumbest thing I ever heard of. What if someone gets hurt?"

Graziella shook her head. "You understand nothing. If someone gets hurt, that is the price. We pay the price."

"You can't mean that. People matter more than ideas."

Graziella put her hands on Percy's cheeks. "You are confused. Sometimes people must be hurt in order to, how do you say, attain a goal. But your confusion is noble." Her hands pressed more firmly. "I cannot afford confusion like yours. Our city is at risk. If we do not stop Expo, everyone gets hurt."

"No way." Percy walked over to the bench and threw himself down, his legs sprawling out in front. "And the *gondole*. I heard everyone talking about the *gondole*. What will happen to them?"

"There will be a strike, if we can, how do you say, *mobilate* them."

"Mobilize."

"If we can mobilize them."

"So the tourists will go home because they can't ride the *gondole*? That's insane. People don't come here just for the *gondole*. They come for the museums and for walking around the canals and alleys."

"They will not walk around if they are afraid of crime."

"All right. The gondola idea, that may be ineffective, but it's all right. No one gets hurt. But the holdup idea is wrong."

Graziella tapped her foot. "You, the *americano*, you will tell Domenico this? And, of course, he will listen." She spoke rapidly, each word a bullet. "Domenico thinks *americani* are to listen to. *Sì, sì.* Yes, *ovviamente,* obviously, oh yes. In fact, you will make him laugh. You with your clever jokes. I see that now. And he will agree with everything you say."

"Okay, he won't listen to me," said Percy, "so you tell him. You know I'm right."

"I know that Venice needs help. I know we must stop Expo." Small wisps of hair had come loose from Graziella's braid at the sides and they flew in different directions with the wind.

Percy had to work to take his attention away from how beautiful she was at that moment. "That's two points. But Domenico had four fingers up. What were the other two plans?"

Graziella looked away. "Similar things."

"What?"

"I cannot tell you now. I see the way you feel."

"People will get hurt?"

"Do not ask questions."

"Graziella, there has to be a better way."

She looked at him and said nothing.

"There has to be a simple, direct, effective way," said Percy.

Graziella squared her shoulders. "Then find it." She waited, and added much more softly, "Please."

CHAPTER 15

On Monday morning the winds were wild.

"Maybe you shouldn't go out to the Porto di Malamocco today." Mom arranged her charcoals in the box, closed it, and drummed her fingers on the lid. "If the canals are this choppy, the sea must be much worse."

"It's our chance, Libby. It's tremendous good luck. They're saying the bora may come, though I can't believe we'd be that lucky." Dad took his raincoat off the hook by the door. "No one thought we'd get a chance to try MOSE until November. But here we are with a mini–summer storm on the way, a perfect trial for the flood-gates. It'll do our troubleshooting for us."

"What if your boat turns over halfway between Giu-decca and the tip of the Lido?"

Dad looked over at Christopher, who sat on the floor with the deck of Italian cards Percy had bought him. He'd been playing with these cards all morning. But now he stopped and watched Mom and Dad as though suspended. Dad smiled at him reassuringly. Christopher didn't smile back. Percy walked over and sat on the floor by Christopher.

"Come on." Dad took Mom by the arm and looked back over his shoulder at Percy. "Grab your brother and bring him along." He led them all into the kitchen and opened the windows that faced the canal. He held Mom close as the wind whipped in past them. "The *vaporetto* is still going up the Rio Nuovo, see it? The Venetians know when a storm is bad. They don't run the boats if it's dangerous." He pulled the windows shut.

"If it gets worse, if it starts to rain . . ."

"I'll turn around and come home."

Mom pressed her lips together in a thin line.

Christopher squeezed Percy's hand. Percy squeezed back.

"Libby, I'll be all right. Chicco's going with me from the CNR. I'll follow his lead." Dad opened a drawer and took out a plastic bag. He put his wallet in it and stuffed it all in his pocket.

Mom stared at him. "Are you trying to make me frantic?"

"Huh?"

"You want them to be able to identify your dead body."

Dad laughed. "I want to keep my cards and money dry if I get splashed in the boat. Listen to me, Lib. The bora doesn't just sweep down without any warning. If it's coming, everyone will know. The radios will announce it. The TV will announce it. There's probably some siren system. There will be time to get home."

Mom nodded doubtfully.

"It's just a windy day so far. That's all. It isn't even raining."

"You're taking your raincoat," said Christopher.

Dad gave Christopher a light rap on the head with his knuckles. "If it rains, I won't get wet." Dad looked quickly at Mom. "I'll be home by four. We'll shop together and make a splendid dinner to celebrate the maiden trial of MOSE." He smiled and left.

Percy took a cloth and wiped the aftermath of breakfast off the kitchen table. "Christopher and I have to get going, Mom. You going to be okay here alone?"

"I don't see why you're going. It'll storm and the children won't have any fun at all." She flopped down into a kitchen chair. "Those priests must be crazy not to shut the program."

"I told you, Mom. Graziella said that if there's really going to be a storm, the whole Estate Ragazzi troop will go out and help everyone prepare."

"How can a bunch of children help prepare for a storm?"

Percy dropped the cloth into the sink. "We'll find out."

"It'll be fun," said Christopher. "It's an adventure."

Mom half-smiled.

"I'll take care of him," said Percy. "Come on, Christopher. Let's get our raincoats."

"Come home if it gets bad," said Mom.

"Of course." Percy kissed his mother on the cheek. Christopher went around the table and kissed her on the other cheek. Then Percy put his raincoat on and Christopher stuffed his into his backpack and they left.

As they went out the gate downstairs, Mom opened the kitchen windows again. "Don't get on any boats," she shouted down.

Percy smiled and waved. "Don't worry."

"And don't walk close to the edge of the *fondamenta*."

"We won't," shouted Percy.

The boys faced into the wind as they crossed the bridge and headed toward the station. Percy had thought maybe the alleys would be deserted. Instead, there were more people than usual. And not just the ordinary people going about their daily business, but old women and old men and kids with packages. Everyone rushed along, intent on an errand. Of course! They were doing all the things they thought they might not get a chance to do for the next few days. It was like the day before a hurricane in Falmouth. Were they all buying batteries and candles? Were they scrubbing their tubs and filling them with water? Were they stashing away canned goods? Percy smiled. Venice wasn't that different from Massachusetts, after all, not today at least.

Christopher pulled on Percy's hand. "The cat's gone."

"What?" Percy leaned down and put his face near Christopher's. "What?"

"The cat that always sleeps on the chair."

"Oh." Percy remembered the brown-and-orange cat that Christopher had shown him the first day he'd gone to the Don Bosco camp.

"He's gone. He's been there every day. But today he's gone."

Percy nodded. "I'm sure he's okay, Christopher. He's just out catting around."

"He knows things are different."

He probably does, thought Percy. "Let's hurry."

They ran over the Scalzi Bridge and up the Lista di Spagna. The tourists didn't seem as thick as usual this morning. Were the hotel proprietors telling them to stay indoors? Percy and Christopher crossed the Ponte delle Guglie and went along the *fondamenta* to the passage that led to the ghetto *campo*. The words EXPO NO, the ones Graziella and Alessandro had painted a week ago, were joined now by other words: LA LOTTA PER LA VITA. ORA! Something for life—now. What was the something? Percy wished he still carried his dictionary around.

They crossed the bridge and hurried into the camp building. Christopher hung his backpack on a hook beside all the others, took out his raincoat, and pulled it on. Then they hurried back outside to the crowd of children gathering outside the church. The *animatori* were grouping them. Graziella was surrounded by ten-year-old girls. She turned from one to the other with energy and excitement.

"Graziella, *ciao*," Percy shouted over the girls' heads.

She looked at him and her smile could have lit up the entire city. *"Ciao, Stracciatella."* A girl pulled on Graziella's arm and she turned away.

Percy wondered about that smile. It seemed carefree. Graziella was obviously riding high. Was she as much turned on by storms as Percy's mother was turned off? "What does *lotta* mean?" shouted Percy over the children's heads.

Graziella looked at him as though he were crazy. But her expression held amusement, too.

"Lotta," shouted Percy. "What does it mean?"

"Fight. Wrestle." She searched for words. "Struggle."

La lotta per la vita. Ora. "Struggle for life. Now." Expo was the death toll for Venice.

"There's my *animatore*," said Christopher. "See you later, Percy."

"No way, Christopher. You're staying by me today."

"But my group is leaving. Look! I'll miss out on everything."

"I promised Mom. You're staying with me. We'll do whatever Graziella's group does."

"Graziella's group?" Christopher shook Percy's arm. "Are you nuts? They're all girls. And look at them. They're big. My group is all six years old, like me. You want me to go with a group of giant girls?"

"Matteo's there."

Christopher looked at the slight figure of Matteo, hanging at the outer edge of the circle of girls around Graziella. "There's eight girls and Matteo." Christopher looked across the group again. "Yup, eight. And I've never talked to him."

"Try. He's okay."

Christopher watched his own group disappear down an alley. "I guess I have no choice."

Percy pushed through the girls and spoke in Graziella's ear. "What's going on?"

"Tables and shutters," she said with a mysterious smile.

"Tables and shutters?"

Graziella laughed. "*Vieni.* Come see." She led the group of children up an alley. Then right and over a bridge and through a tunnel and left again. They went down a long *fondamenta* by a narrow canal and came out at the wide walk that led down to the Fondamenta Nuove boat

187

stop. Graziella went into the first shop on the lagoon side while Percy and Christopher waited outside with the girls and Matteo. Matteo stood beside Percy, their arms brushing. The girls were surprisingly quiet. They huddled in groups of two and three and their eyes darted to the shop door every few minutes.

"Va bene. I tavoli sono all'indietro. Venite, ragazzi." Graziella waved the children through the shop door to the rear of the store. "The tables are at the back," she said, snaking her way between Percy and Matteo and taking the boy's hand. She glowed up at Percy. "Help us carry them."

"What tables? And what are you so happy about?"

But Graziella had pulled ahead with Matteo and didn't answer.

They went into a dimly lit storage room. In one corner was a tall stack of wooden tables that stood on legs no more than two feet high. Graziella went to one end of the tables and called for help. *"Aiutami."* Percy took the other end. They lifted a table off the stack. Two girls took it from them and headed out of the store. They lifted off the second table and two more girls took it away. They kept lifting tables and the children kept coming in pairs and taking them away. Christopher stood aside at first. But when Matteo charged ahead confidently, he followed. The two boys were a team. Then Percy and Graziella carried the last table out together.

They set the last table inside near the shop door. Then they went out onto the *fondamenta*. Now Percy could see where all the other tables had gone. They were lined up along the wall, going from shop to shop. And inside each shop door you could see one table waiting. It began to make sense. "To walk on if the water comes over the *fondamenta*."

Graziella smiled. *"Bravo!"* She tugged teasingly at Percy's sleeve.

"And inside each shop there's one more that the shopkeeper will put outside the door when the time comes."

She clapped her hands. *"Bravissimo!"*

Percy smiled. "So you really think it's going to storm that bad?"

Graziella nodded.

"The bora?"

"Sì." Graziella gave a deep sigh of satisfaction. "The blessed bora."

Percy couldn't help smiling at her. "A storm is coming and you're smiling your ass off. I don't get it."

Graziella looked down over her shoulder questioningly. "Smiling my ass off?"

"It's an expression. Your ass is still there, thank heavens."

Graziella gave him a peck on the cheek. "This storm,

189

the bora, she saves my home." Her hands flew around happily as she talked. "She means I do not have to move, maybe."

Percy grinned at her expressive hands. He caught them in his own. "What are you talking about? What's this about moving?"

"If Expo comes to Venice, housing prices go up even more. I told you. When my grandmother dies, we lose that home. I will not be allowed to stay in the public housing unless I am already married and my husband is *gondoliere* by then. And if I have to leave that home, I cannot find another I can afford in Venice, not the tiniest apartment, if Expo comes. But the bora will keep Expo out. The bora will let me stay in Venice." Graziella slipped free of Percy and turned to the children. *"Sbrighiamoci!"* Then she smiled down at Christopher. "Let us hurry. We have much left to do."

Percy followed slowly. He thought of Graziella's home, her grandmother's room, the smell of the flowers, the breeze through the lace curtains, how peaceful he had felt there. He thought of the mystery of the alleys at night and the glory of morning sunlight on the lagoon and the sweet and sour smells of the markets and restaurants. All of that was the Venice Percy was learning to love. He hadn't realized all of that was in danger of being lost. If Expo came. So it wasn't totally political, after all—this fight of

Graziella's against Expo. Her personal life was precarious. She should have told him sooner—he would have understood her better. But, in fact, he didn't understand her now. How would the storm keep Expo from coming? He had to ask.

But Graziella was all business, talking to shopkeepers and telling the children what to do. She barely looked at Percy, except to give him a radiant smile and rush along. All of them spent the next two hours carting tables out of storage rooms and lining them up along the *fondamenta* and alleys. They raced around in a frenzy. Suddenly Graziella looked at her watch and herded them all back to Don Bosco.

Graziella spoke quickly to the children. Then she turned to Christopher. "If you come back after lunch, we'll close shutters. But be here early—around two."

"Go from house to house?" asked Christopher.

"*Sì.*" Graziella smiled. "*Una preghiera contro il mare.* A prayer against the sea. That is how much the shutters help." She laughed. "They do not work at all." She looked up and gave Percy a face so full of joy, he was stunned.

Percy smiled back in confusion. "I don't understand at all. How does a storm keep out Expo?"

"Venice will have high water."

"High water." That was what people called a flood

here, Percy knew—but it sounded special the way she said it. He liked the way she said it. "But isn't high water awful? Anyway, there won't be any high water."

"Yes there will. The bora comes, I feel it in my bones. Venice will be under water within a day. Maybe even tonight."

"The bora may come," said Percy, "but Venice won't be under water."

"Yes it will. And that is the beautiful thing. The most beautiful beautiful thing."

Christopher hopped on one foot. "High water is beautiful?"

"High water will show them that Venice cannot be trusted. Venice is not the perfect tourist city all summer. Venice can have high water, and tourists will go away. The committee will vote not to give Venice Expo after all." She laughed. "It is the answer to a prayer." She looked lovingly at Percy and then back at Christopher. "And it is an answer that even your big brother can accept. Oh, lovely water will come in from the Adriatic and cover this *fondamenta,* this one right here, where we stand."

"No it won't," said Christopher, jumping to a halt right in front of Graziella. "I don't know about all the other things you said. But I know about the Adriatic. My father talks about the Adriatic all the time. My father won't let the water come in from the Adriatic."

Graziella tousled Christopher's hair. "Do not worry, Cristoforo, the high water will not hurt you."

Percy put his hand on top of Graziella's and held hers still. He shook his head. "No." He swallowed hard. "Oh, Graziella. MOSE is in place. The floodgates. The floodgates, don't you see? They're the reason my family is here this summer. I never told you, I guess. My father's a civil engineer—he worked on their design. He's sure they'll work. And Venice will never have high water again."

Graziella stared at Percy. The joy drained from her face.

CHAPTER 16

"Have a *tramezzino,* boys. On the kitchen table." Mom perched on the arm of the couch. Her eyes were fixed on the TV weatherman.

Christopher raced into the kitchen, leaving Percy standing in the hall watching his mother. Seated like that, with all her attention on the news, she seemed more connected to this world than usual. He had a momentary impulse to talk to her. Get her perspective on things. This whole business with Expo made him anxious. The storm would come and MOSE would hold back the high water and Graziella's politico friends would be desperate and they'd start holding up bars and who knew what else. And maybe Graziella would consider Percy the enemy, since his father helped with MOSE. Percy wanted to talk to his mother.

But, actually, he knew what Mom would say. She'd be horrified at the idea of holdups.

Percy was horrified at the idea of holdups.

And then she might try to stop him from seeing Graziella.

Forget talking.

"Looks spooky," said Christopher. "Come in here, Percy. You better try them first."

Percy went into the kitchen and glanced at the plate of little half sandwiches on thin white bread, cut on the diagonal to make triangles. They were fat in the middle with various colors peeking out. "Spooky, yeah." He picked one up. A blob of pickled artichoke coated in mayonnaise squished out onto his hand. He licked it off. "Good, though."

Christopher picked up one that had hardboiled egg and tomato slices. "Is this all there is to eat?" he called out.

"Yes," Mom called back.

Christopher took a bite and followed Percy back into the living room.

"So what's the story?" Percy sat on the couch and looked at the weather map on the TV. The border between Italy and Slovenia was covered with red arrows. A man stood beside the map and gesticulated wildly. Percy tried his best to understand, but the guy spoke too fast. Tension tightened Percy's whole body. "What're they saying?"

"I'm not sure. It seems a wind is circling in the mountains of Slovenia and no one knows if it will come this way, but everyone's preparing. They showed a videotape of Trieste. People there are nailing windows shut and putting cement blocks in their Fiats so they won't get blown over." Mom got up and turned off the TV.

"Hey, I wanted to see."

"There's nothing to see. No one has decided whether Venice should be alarmed yet or not. And I'm sick of hearing it."

Percy shook his head in annoyance. "I was watching."

"What does it matter?" Mom looked at him quizzically. "You can't understand the announcer anyway."

"We put out tables," said Christopher.

"Tables?"

Percy nodded irritably. "Tables, that's what he said." Mom looked baffled. Percy spoke sharply, as if she was an idiot: "For people to walk on if there's high water."

"You're certainly moody."

"Look who's talking," Percy snapped back.

Mom put her hands to her cheeks. "Percy? Are you okay?"

"Sorry," mumbled Percy. Mom stood by the coffee table and looked at him. Then she looked down at her drawing pad. She rubbed her upper arms and shivered. Her skirt hung limp around her slight body. Percy felt an urge of remorse and protectiveness. "I am sorry, Mom. I've got things on my mind."

"Want to talk?"

Percy wavered for an instant. "Later, maybe."

Mom nodded. "Okay. Does the water in the canals look any worse?"

"No." Percy finished his sandwich. "I'm going to get another of these. What did you call them?"

"*Tramezzino*. Something to snack on between meals. What was in yours?"

"A bunch of gooshy little marinated things. Artichokes and mushrooms and maybe eggplants."

"That's *alla zingara*," said Mom. "It means 'the Gypsy woman's way.'" She picked up a charcoal and squatted by the blank sheet of white paper in the open drawing pad on the coffee table, getting that concentration on her face that always preceded a burst of drawing. Then she stood up quickly, walked around the coffee table, sat on the couch, and pulled the drawing pad onto her lap. She sketched something curved and bulky. "Gypsy woman," she muttered.

A Gypsy woman. *Zingara*. Graziella was sure no Gypsy woman. Venice was so much her home that she could never feel at peace anywhere else. All the peace and joy and light and love in her universe was centered in Venice.

"I hate these sandwiches," said Christopher.

"Oh, well," said Mom, without looking up from her pad, "think of the nutrition." Mom's sketch was now recognizable as a boat. "Where do you think your father is now?"

"He's all right, Mom." Percy pivoted on the couch arm so that he could look over his mother's shoulder more easily. She was in her element. Competent. Creative. "Mom, I think maybe I do want to talk to you about something."

"Hmmm?" she said distractedly.

"I want a banana," said Christopher.

"Go get one, then." Percy lifted his heels off the floor so that only his toes touched. He bounced his knees. "And grab me another *tramezzino*."

"I wish your father was in charge of the Porto di Lido instead of the Malamocco." The charcoal in Mom's fingers snapped in half. She let it slide onto her lap while she picked up a pencil. "The Malamocco is the deepest channel from the Adriatic. I think he likes having the most dangerous assignments." She drew carvings along the boat's side.

Percy had been wrong; Mom wasn't strong now. She was drawing to keep herself from jumping out of her skin. "Stop worrying," he said gently. He felt jittery himself. He turned on the TV. An old American western was showing. He changed channels. Another weather map, another half-crazed-looking weatherman. Percy turned to his mother. "Are they saying anything new?"

"Shhh." Mom leaned forward. "I think . . . no, I'm not sure. They're just as mealymouthed as before. No one knows what's going on. Turn it off."

Percy turned off the TV. "Hurry up, Christopher, we've got to go."

Christopher came in with a peach in one hand and a *tramezzino alla zingara* in the other. "No bananas," he said, squeezing the peach a little. He handed the sandwich to Percy.

"It's early yet. Don't go," said Mom.

"I want to." Percy took his raincoat off the hook and put it on. Christopher watched in silence. Then he did the same.

"Percy, didn't you say you wanted to talk about something?"

"Later, Mom. I said later."

"Wait." Mom wandered back to the couch and plopped down onto it as though she had no energy. She pulled her drawing pad back onto her lap.

Percy waited. Mom kept drawing. "Mom? Hey, Mom? Why'd you ask us to wait?"

"Percy . . ."

"What, Mom?"

"Christopher . . ."

"What, Mom?"

"Don't forget me."

Percy threw his hands up. "You know, Mom, you say the craziest things." How could he have ever thought of confiding in her?

Christopher kissed his mother on the cheek, careful not to disturb her drawing. "I'll never forget you. I love you."

Percy cleared his throat. "I love you, too, Mom. Bye." He closed the door as quietly as he could. Then he wolfed down the sandwich as they raced for the stairs. It was still dry out, but the wind had picked up. They headed down the *fondamenta* along the Rio Nuovo, moving quickly.

"What's the rush?" shouted Christopher into the wind. He grabbed the back of Percy's raincoat. "Why are we running? There won't be anyone there yet when we get to Don Bosco."

"We're going somewhere else first."

"Where?"

Percy took Christopher's hand and pulled him close. They passed their usual bridge without crossing it. They went over the left bridge of the three that came together at the corner known as the Tre Ponti. At the first alley they turned onto the wide avenue that Percy had discovered on his solitary walk two weeks ago. Less than two weeks ago. He hadn't even known Graziella's name then.

A boy of maybe twelve stood under a tree in the avenue and watched Percy and Christopher approach. A woman opened a shutter, yelled at the boy, and pulled it shut again. The boy smirked and said confidingly to Percy, *"Stronza."* He shrugged and went into the building.

"That's their *f*-word," said Christopher.

"Their *f*-word?" Percy squeezed Christopher's hand. "Is that what they taught you to call it in kindergarten?"

"Yup. Bad words are *f*-words."

"Well, not exactly. An *f*-word has to start with *f*. The *f* sound is *fffff*."

"Oh." Christopher put his top teeth on his bottom lip and made the sound *fffff*. "Yeah, you're right."

They passed the prison and stopped at the bridge with the locked electric gate. Percy looked up and down the canal.

"Are we waiting for Graziella?" Christopher asked.

Percy smiled. "How'd you guess?" He jammed his fists into his pockets and looked around. "Where could she be?"

"Maybe she's putting out more tables in case of high water."

"Yeah." Percy blew air out between his lips. "She's still praying for a flood."

"A flood? Who said anything about a flood?"

Percy looked at Christopher. "That's what we prepared for all morning."

Christopher's face went slack. "Is high water the same as a flood?"

"Yeah. Of course."

"When there's a flood, children die," said Christopher slowly.

"No they don't." Percy drew back and looked down at Christopher with genuine surprise. "What a dumb thing to say."

"They die." Christopher stood tall. He looked stricken.

Percy took his hand. "Everyone lives on the second floor or higher. The water never reaches that high. It only goes a few inches deep on the first floor—maybe a foot at most."

"They drown."

Percy tugged on Christopher's fingers one by one. "Who told you that? Only a very little child could drown in water a few inches deep, and very little children are near their parents all the time—so their parents won't let them drown."

"It's kids my age that drown," said Christopher. "They walk along the *fondamenta* and don't know where it ends, 'cause of the water, and they fall off into a canal and they die."

It sounded right. Percy squeezed Christopher's hand. "You won't die, Christopher. You aren't stupid enough to fall into a canal. Anyway, MOSE's going to work and it's not going to flood. And, anyway, who even knows if the storm is going to come? All this worrying could be over nothing."

Christopher's eyes brimmed.

"Look!" Percy pointed to a green fruit boat that had just entered the canal from another, smaller one about fifty yards up. Crates of fruit were piled three deep on both sides of the boat.

They ran along the *fondamenta* and Graziella steered the boat to the edge and threw Percy a rope. "*Venite. Subito.* Come on."

Percy held the rope and stared at her. "I can't bring Christopher onto a boat in this weather. He can hardly swim."

Graziella climbed out of the boat and took the rope from Percy. She tied it to a post stuck into the canal right at the edge of the *fondamenta*. "We can sit in the boat and talk." She smiled at Christopher. "It is safe. We are tied up. And Matteo is here, too. He came home for lunch with me, because there was not enough time to go all the way back to Giudecca today."

"I don't see Matteo," said Christopher.

Matteo's face peeked out from behind a stack of crates. He smiled, then came all the way out.

Christopher turned around suddenly. "Hey, Percy." He pointed at Matteo's backpack. "I left my backpack at Don Bosco."

"We'll get it later."

"I want it now."

"Later, Christopher. I promise."

Christopher pushed his lips out. But he turned around and got onto the boat with Percy behind him. They walked down the narrow path between the walls of fruit crates. Graziella sat on the floor of the boat. Percy sat beside her, while Christopher nestled in near Matteo.

"Your father works for the CNR," said Graziella.

"That's right," said Percy. "How'd you find out?"

"Alessandro asked people when I told him why your father was here."

Percy gave a harumphing laugh. "Do you have spies at the CNR?"

"You could say that."

The boat rocked uneasily. The water slapped at its sides. "So?" said Percy. "What now?"

"One thing. That is all you have to do for us."

Percy looked at Graziella.

"A set of plans of MOSE. We need a set of plans."

Percy shook his head. "You want me to steal from my father?" He shook his head again. "You're planning to sabotage MOSE. You must be crazy."

"This is the uncrazy way."

"Wow, I don't want to hear about the crazy way." Percy sighed. "I would never steal from my father."

Graziella didn't blink.

Christopher stood up and leaned against the fruit crates. The boat rocked harder. His face was drawn; he was obviously seasick.

"I have to get Christopher off this boat," said Percy.

Graziella took Percy's hand and held tight. She turned to Christopher. "*Attenzione*. Be careful. Do not fall." Then she looked back at Percy. "If we understand how MOSE works, we can stop it."

"My father has spent years working on MOSE. Literally years."

"And I have lived my whole life in a city that is going to die unless you help us."

"No." Percy pulled his hand away. "I couldn't help you, Graziella, even if I was willing, which I'm not. I've been through every detail with my dad. We sit around sometimes troubleshooting the system. Nothing can stop MOSE."

Graziella shook her head violently. "That is not true. There is always a way to stop things."

Percy didn't answer.

"I think I'm going to be sick," said Christopher. He leaned over and vomited on his shoes.

CHAPTER 17

"I ruined my *marcialunghe*," said Christopher. He stepped out of his shoes without touching them by pressing the toe of one foot against the heel of the other.

Mom picked up the *marcialunghe* between the tips of her thumb and index finger. "I'll rinse them off and pop them in the washing machine." She wrinkled her nose. "Malodorous."

Christopher wrinkled his nose. "Does that mean the same as *schifoso*?"

"*Schifoso*," said Matteo. "*Assolutamente schifoso.*" He had come home with them because the water was getting too rough for him to stay in the boat. Graziella was supposed to tell a cousin of his to stop by later for him.

Mom laughed at Matteo. Then she turned to Christopher. "You certainly have picked up a lot of Italian." She guided Christopher into the bathroom while Percy and Matteo followed close behind. "*Schifoso* means something is disgusting. *Malodorous* means something stinks." She dropped the *marcialunghe* in the sink and turned on the faucet. "Percy, go get the liquid detergent in the kitchen. Your brother needs a bubble bath."

The TV was still on in the living room. Percy glanced at the screen. Had the red arrows multiplied on the weather map? He went into the kitchen, stuffed the last *tramezzino* into his mouth—tuna salad with hardboiled egg and tons of mayonnaise—and grabbed the liquid detergent. He ran back with it and squeezed some into the filling tub.

"What're you eating?" said Christopher.

"*Tramezzino,*" mumbled Percy through a full mouth.

"I'm hungry," said Christopher. "I want real food." He looked at Matteo. "Matteo wants real food, too."

Matteo smiled cooperatively at the mention of his name, completely undisturbed by the incomprehensibility of English. He picked up the bar of soap and floated it in the tub water.

Mom leaned with her back against the tiled wall and her arms crossed at her chest. "I wonder if I should call Caterina. She's all alone and blind and I bet she's worried. I'm going to call her."

"We want food," said Christopher loudly. "We're starving. Mom, we're starving."

"Food," said Mom. "Oh, well, I could send Percy out for a pizza, I suppose."

"Pizza," said Matteo softly.

"Percy can't go out in the storm," said Christopher.

"It won't really storm for hours yet. And Percy doesn't have to get on any boats to buy a pizza." Mom leaned over and squirted bubble bath into the tub. "How about one of those pizzas with four cheeses?"

"I've got to get back to Don Bosco," said Percy.

"And Italian pizza is malodorous," said Christopher.

"Malodorous?" said Mom.

"Yeah, it stinks. It's got lousy crust."

"No, that's not how you use the word . . ."

"You said it," said Christopher belligerently. "You said it and now you say it's something else." He got into the tub and floated the soap bar back toward Matteo. "Italian is easier, you know that? People always tell me how good I am when I say anything in Italian. I think I'm staying here forever."

Percy slid his hands into the back pockets of his jeans. "I've got to go, Mom. Thanks for watching out for Matteo."

Mom nodded at Percy. Then she patted Christopher's head. "Maybe you'll come live in Venice when you're big. I could come visit you. You could ferry me about in your gondola."

"It doesn't work that way, Mom," said Percy with sudden harshness. "You can't be a *gondoliere* unless you have a license. And you can't get a license unless you inherit it. And Christopher wouldn't ever come live in Venice anyway because there are no jobs here. You can't live a decent life in Venice unless you act like a slave to the tourists. Don't put stupid ideas in his head. Don't go ruining his life."

"My goodness, Percy." Mom looked at Percy with amazement. "What on earth was that speech all about?"

"There's no future here. Venice isn't for young people like Christopher. Like me. It isn't for anyone in their right mind."

"It's a living museum, Percy."

"No, it's a dead museum, Mom."

Mom's mouth hung open.

Percy knew it wasn't fair to jump on her like that. He wanted to apologize but, still, "I've got to go," he said, and ran into the hall. He grabbed his raincoat and left.

The air was full of water. Not an outright, honest drizzle, just a warm wetness that coated Percy's cheeks and made his breathing feel heavy and fecund, as though something were going to breed in his trachea. And then the wind stopped. Percy looked at the flat waters of the canals, baffled for a moment. All motion had stopped. It hadn't died down gradually; it had ceased suddenly. The stillness was eerie.

Percy pulled on his raincoat as he raced along the empty

fondamenta and over one of the Tre Ponti, back along the wide avenue, past the prison, to the narrow canal where Graziella was waiting in the fruit boat. Only she wasn't alone now.

"Salve," called Alessandro from the other bank of the canal.

The boat was now attached to a pole on the far side, and a man in the boat lifted up a full crate of fruit and handed it to Alessandro. The man turned to Percy with an anxious face. It was Claudio, the guy he'd met on the night of the fireworks. *"Ciao."*

"Ciao," said Percy. *"Ciao, ciao."* Alessandro walked down an alley with the fruit crate.

Graziella appeared at Percy's side. "Come with me. We must put the fruit in the warehouse." She led him to the gate and inserted her key. The gate slowly swung open with a whirring noise. Graziella and Percy crossed the bridge and went over to the boat just as Alessandro returned.

"Ecco," said Claudio. He held up a crate of bananas.

Percy took the crate. Alessandro took another crate, and Percy followed him down the alley and through a low door. They stacked the crates inside. The four of them lugged all the crates one by one into the warehouse.

Alessandro nodded to Percy. *"Grazie. In bocca al lupo."*

Claudio shook Percy's hand. *"Grazie. Ci vediamo, eh?"* The two men left.

Percy sat down on a ledge on the side of the boat and pulled Graziella onto his lap. He laced his fingers through hers. "What was that all about? What did they say to me?"

"Claudio said he would see you again later. And Alessandro wished you luck. *'In bocca al lupo.'* It means in the mouth of the wolf. We do not wish luck directly. It is . . . part of . . . oh, *scaramanzia.*"

"Scaramanzia?"

"It is difficult to explain. A kind of superstition. You say the opposite, to make the bad thing not happen."

"Sure," said Percy, "I get it." He wrapped his arms around Graziella. "But I don't get it really. Why do I need luck?"

"We all need luck."

A light drizzle had begun while they were unloading the boat. Percy turned his face upward and shut his eyes. Luck. People needed luck when they were doing something risky. Claudio and Alessandro were doing something risky. "Where did they go?"

Graziella didn't answer.

Percy opened his eyes and studied Graziella. "Does it have something to do with MOSE?"

"Yes."

Percy swallowed. "Whatever they're planning, it won't work. The sections of the floodgate are made of steel and they are invulnerable. Even if something huge—something like the hull of some wrecked ship or whatever—got swept up along the sea floor, the gate would just crush it. It's gigantic."

"They do not plan to break the floodgate." Graziella looked steadily at Percy. "There is a much more simple way. Simple, direct, effective, like you said." She spoke slowly and deliberately. "Something that takes just pulling a lever."

Percy shook his head. What then? And suddenly it hit him. "They're going to the transformers by the floodgates. That's it, isn't it? They're going to cut off the electricity."

"It is a good plan, no? Nothing gets destroyed. Your father's project can continue after the flood, after Venice has lost Expo."

"No, it isn't a good plan. No, no, no." Percy pushed away from Graziella and stood up. "Floods are dangerous. People get sick. Children drown. How can you be so irresponsible?"

Graziella didn't flinch. She spoke without feeling, almost automatically. "I told you before: We pay the price. Venice must be saved."

"You're out of your mind. I don't understand politics." Percy walked along the *fondamenta* fast now.

Graziella ran beside him. "Where are you going?"

"To stop them, of course."

"You cannot stop them."

"Just watch."

"You are angry."

212

"You got it. Graziella, look, I want to help you. But you're doing this all wrong."

Graziella took his arm. "Do not say that. You are the one who makes mistake. You cannot stop them and you should not stop them."

Percy pulled his arm away. "There's no time to talk." He ran. He passed a neighborhood cafe exuding the sweet smells of sardines and onions in vinegar. Normally he loved that smell, but now it turned his stomach. He didn't stop running till he got to the Zattere. The *vaporetto* wasn't in yet. He looked around frantically. There was a public phone right outside Nico's *gelateria*. Good. He'd be gone for hours and who knew when he'd get the chance to telephone again? He couldn't leave his mother worrying that long.

Percy felt in his pocket. No change. Oh no.

A hand squeezed his shoulder. Percy turned to face Graziella. She said, "You want to make a telephone call? Who do you call?"

"My mother. She worries."

Graziella held out a coin.

Percy took it and dropped it in the telephone. "I'm going to stop them, Graziella." He dialed.

Graziella stood beside him and looked out over the canal.

"Pronto."

"Hi, Mom."

"Oh, Percy, thank heavens. Where are you?"

"I just wanted to tell you I won't be home for a while, so don't worry."

"What are you talking about? The storm's coming. It's really coming, Percy. They said it."

"It won't hit for hours, Mom."

"The weather report changed right after you left. You should have stopped to listen to a radio. Come home. All of you. Right now."

All of him? What? "I can't. Is Dad there?"

"No."

"Do you have a phone number for him?"

"No. He's out someplace."

Wow. That meant Percy was on his own. "All right. Bye, Mom. Don't worry about me." The *vaporetto* was pulling up to the boat stop. "I've got to go now."

"Don't go anywhere. They're saying the storm will last through the evening, at the very least. Bring Christopher and Matteo back here immediately. Immediately, Percy."

Percy clutched the phone tight. "What did you say? Aren't they there?"

"You mean they're not with you?"

"No, Mom."

"They disappeared." Mom's voice cracked. "I called Caterina and she wanted me to come over and secure the shutters. I was only gone twenty minutes. I told them not to move! When I got back, they weren't here. I thought they went to meet you."

"Oh, God." People shoved onto the boat. "I'm going, Mom." Percy hung up the phone. He grabbed Graziella by the hand.

Graziella pulled back.

"Come on!"

"I'm not going with you."

"You have to. I need your help."

"I won't help you. My city needs my help."

"Matteo and Christopher left the apartment. My mother doesn't know where they are. They'll be out in the storm, Graziella."

Graziella's fingers tightened around Percy's. "Matteo knows enough to get out of a storm."

"Are you sure? And what about Christopher? He's six, Graziella. He doesn't know what to do in a flood."

Graziella's face went slack. She shook her head slowly. Then she whispered, "Okay." And now she looked at him hard and her eyes came alive all at once. "Okay, yes. I'll help you stop Alessandro and Claudio."

"Do you want to call your grandmother?" asked Percy.

"She is too deaf for the telephone." Graziella was pulling Percy now. They ran for the boat, which was already packed. "Claudio and Alessandro, they went to the Porto di Malamocco."

Percy nodded as they pushed their way into the boat. "They're smart. That's the deepest channel. If the flood-gate fails at Malamocco, it won't matter if it works at the Porto di Lido and the Porto di Chioggia." He shook his head. "They're too smart for their own good."

"We can take the bus from Lido to Alberoni. If we make the right, how do you say, *coincidenza*—connection, yes, we will be there in time."

Percy looked around. His eyes settled on the conductor. "No tickets," whispered Percy in Graziella's ear.

"I have them."

"We didn't stamp them."

She gave a clipped, almost sad laugh. "I hope that is our smallest problem today. Besides, no one checks in a storm."

The boat was halfway across the water when the true rains came. It was a steady drumming. Within minutes the sea had changed complexion entirely. It went from deep blue to creamy blue, flecked with the white foam that tipped the waves.

"Un mare mosso," said a woman beside Percy. She rubbed her fingers together nervously.

Graziella wrapped both her arms around Percy's right arm and held herself close to him. She shivered in the warm rain. "The sea is agitated," she whispered in his ear. "But it is not bad yet."

By the time they reached the Lido, no one could say the

sea was not bad yet. The waves splashed over the floating wooden platform where they were to disembark. With each wave the *vaporetto* slammed into the tires on the side of the platform. The people behind Percy and Graziella pushed to get off the boat. A kind of near-hysteria electrified the air. At last the ticket takers opened the boat chain and two conductors gave people a hand from both sides as they poured out of the boat. The woman beside Percy slipped and fell. She had already been stepped on by several people before he managed to pull her upright again. She brushed at her clothes frantically and hurried off.

Behind the restraining chain on the platform an even larger crowd waited to get back to Venice. But three other conductors were deep in angry discussion in front of the chain. The ticket seller in the booth pushed his way through the crowd and joined the discussion. It was as dark as early evening, though it was just two-thirty.

"Chiuso!" called out one conductor finally. *"Finito!"*

People shouted. Someone pushed down the conductor who had made the announcement. A group of people circled him and pulled him up.

Percy realized with shock that the conductor had just decided to stop all the boats. He and Graziella were lucky to have gotten here before the boats shut down. But how would they get back?

Percy and Graziella passed by the fracas and headed up the avenue that went straight to the beaches on the seaward side of the island. The street lamps had turned on. A small crowd gathered at the bus stop across from the Standa department store. The people seemed to merge into one blue-green mass in the thick sheets of rain that now came down as an ominous roar. Graziella walked up to the pole at the stop and strained to read the schedule through the rain. "Five, six minutes," she shouted to Percy. "That is all."

Five minutes passed. Then another. The crowd grew.

"Finalmente," shouted Graziella, pointing.

The bus sent up a thick spray as it rolled into the water that already rushed along the curbs several inches deep. Holding hands tightly, Percy and Graziella let themselves be pushed on. They stood in the center of the bus, their free hands hanging on to a strap. The bus lurched forward, turned a corner, and started on the long trek to Alberoni, at the other end of the island. People got off periodically. The gray rain enveloped them immediately. Few got on. Now and then a car passed in one direction or the other and the bus driver veered to the right. But most of the time they just moved, slowly and inexorably, up the center of the road.

"Do not worry. The Lido goes under water long before Venice does." Graziella's eyes stayed fixed on the road ahead, though it was nearly impossible to see anything out the front windshield from where they were. Her shirt and pants stuck to her body and a puddle formed around both their feet. No one on the bus talked. Percy had the sense of being sealed in, traveling through territories of unknown dangers, like a space traveler.

The thunder rolled now. Percy leaned across the people in the seat he stood beside and looked out the window. The road was lined with small well-lit homes that seemed undaunted by the storm. Lightning flashed almost immediately. Another thunder roll. And the bus driver unexpectedly turned off the one and only road that ran the whole distance of the island. They passed under an arched sign with giant lettering. Percy could make out MOROSINI.

The bus driver stopped and turned off the engine. He slapped his hands back and forth as though he was wiping off sand. *"È troppo pericoloso. Ci fermiamo qui."* He pushed a button and the doors opened with a hiss. He left the bus.

"Where are we?"

Graziella shook her head. "It is a camp run by the Morosini priests. I used to play here in the summer when I was small." She bit her bottom lip. "He says it is too dangerous to go on. But that means it is too dangerous for the bus. Not for us. We are close now—almost to the cemetery at the end of the island. We can walk the rest of the way."

They got out and the last few passengers ran into the sand-colored building, while Percy and Graziella headed back to the main road. They walked in the street because the ditch on either side was now a running stream. Up ahead the lights in the windows of the houses seemed to beckon. They ran. It was still light enough to see the road, but the road was slippery and full of holes hidden under long puddles. They went through the tiny village of Alberoni and slowed to a fast walk. The cemetery couldn't have been more than a hundred yards away when suddenly the lights went out everywhere, all of them, all at once. Lightning flashed. Thunder boomed.

Percy pulled Graziella behind him up under the last carport. "The electricity is out. The whole area is blacked out."

Graziella looked stunned. "Oh! It does not matter now. The floodgate cannot work, no matter what. Oh!" Her eyes filled with tears.

CHAPTER 18

"I've got to get back to Venice." Percy could hardly think.

Graziella put her knuckles to her mouth and bit down. "No more boats run now." She shook her head crazily. "No more boats."

Percy looked around. There were no people in any direction. Nothing alive except one lone gull clinging to a rock. It kept shifting directions.

"Poor bird," said Graziella, pointing to the gull. "It must face into the wind, but the wind shifts. The wind shifts. *Ahime! O Dio.*" She kept shaking her head. "But someone will help them. Someone must help them. In Venice everyone helps in high water."

Percy stared at the water. "If it's this wild in the lagoon, imagine what it's like on the seaward side."

"This is not so severe," said Graziella. "No. I have seen the waves higher than six meters. It will be a small flood. Matteo and Christopher will be fine."

Percy held Graziella tight. The warmth of her body radiated through her wet clothes. He wanted to believe her. He wanted to hold her forever.

Graziella spoke into his shoulder. "There is a restaurant. We must get out of the storm. This way." She led Percy by the hand through the blinding rain. Soon they stumbled onto a wood porch and into the restaurant entrance. They stood dripping.

A short, heavyset man with glasses and a tonsure of black hair rushed up. *"Accomodatevi."* The man spouted rapid Venetian at them while he ushered them into the empty dining room.

A thin woman with a worried smile came into the room—then left quickly. She was back in a flash and handed them each a towel.

Graziella and Percy mumbled, *"Grazie,"* repeatedly.

The man talked briefly with Graziella. Then he and his wife went back to work. They raced around the dining hall, he carrying chairs by twos up the stairs in the rear and she collecting the tiny dishes of salt and pepper and the vinegar bottles from the tables and setting them on high shelves against the wall.

Percy snapped to attention. He needed to be busy or he'd go mad with worry. Like Mom. There was not a thing he could do to help Christopher and Matteo now. He picked up two chairs and headed for the stairs, following the man. Graziella came alive at the same instant. She swept a tablecloth off the nearest table, folded it, and ran for the shelves.

After the chairs came the tables: They turned over every other table and set it upside down on the one nearest it. The woman cleared out the shelves under the cash register. The man surveyed the scene, nodded, then went and sat at the only table they had not disturbed. It was right in front of the only window that wasn't yet shuttered. And four chairs waited there.

The woman put an open bottle of wine on the table and a basket of skinny doughnut-shaped white things. *"Niente cena stasera,"* she said.

"No dinner tonight," whispered Graziella. *"Grazie, signora."*

"Grazie," echoed Percy. *"Mille grazie, signora. E molto molto gentile."* He thought about the 20,000 lire in his pocket—it would pay for practically nothing. He whispered to Graziella, "How much does it cost?"

"If you mention money, they will be offended. In a storm, everyone takes in people."

That was good to know. Someone must have taken in Christopher and Matteo. Oh, yes.

"We can sit here and watch the storm until it becomes too dangerous. Then we'll go upstairs." Graziella picked up one of the doughnuts and gnawed at it distractedly. "*Bussolai*. These are island breads of these people. They go back centuries."

Percy took a bite. It crunched away into powder. "I can believe that," he said with a laugh that came out a lot louder than he intended.

Graziella smiled ruefully. "Do not joke about tradition."

"Wouldn't think of it."

Graziella turned to the woman and they got into a lively conversation.

Percy gave up trying to follow the Italian. He stuck another of the *bussolai* into his mouth. It was soothing. He sucked on it till it was soft, then chewed and swallowed. Graziella was still talking.

Percy stood up. *"Dov'è il telefono, per favore?"*

The woman took a candle in a holder off a shelf, lit the candle, and led him down a dark corridor. Halfway down was a phone on a small table. *"Eccolo, signore."*

"Grazie." Percy dialed.

The woman left the candle with him and went back to the dining hall.

"Pronto," said Percy's father in his thick American accent.

"Hi, Dad," Percy said with relief. Dad had made it home, at least.

"Where are you?"

"At a restaurant on the Lido."

"What? Are you crazy?"

"Have the boys come back?" asked Percy.

"No. I just came in. I looked everywhere."

Percy's heart did a flop. He heard a little scuffle on the other end of the phone.

Mom's voice came on. "You're on the Lido, Percy? Oh, come home when you can."

"I'll be on the first boat that comes back to Venice, Mom."

"No, no, no. Take the second boat. Make sure the first one doesn't sink before you step on one."

Percy laughed in spite of himself. "Okay, Mom."

"Be careful."

"Yeah, Mom."

"I'm going out to look for the boys again now," she said.

Dad got back on the phone. "Do you have any money on you?"

Percy gulped. "Plenty, Dad."

"Who will take you in? Where will you sleep?"

"It's all taken care of."

"Just get home safe."

"Okay, Dad. Dad?"

"What?"

"The boys are going to show up."

"Of course they are."

"Bye." Percy hung up. He walked through the dark corridor back to the dining room. The man was standing at the window now. Percy stood beside him. Christopher and Matteo were somewhere in this wind and rain, if they hadn't yet found shelter.

Graziella got up and stood beside him. "Did the boys come home?"

"Not yet."

"They will be okay," Graziella said firmly. "And we will take the first boat back to Venice after the storm."

"We can't. I promised Mom I wouldn't take the first boat."

"Why not?"

"She wants to make sure it's safe. She said to take the second."

Graziella gave a tiny smile. "I want to meet this mother."

"You will."

"Guardate," said the man. He pointed his finger off to the left. *"Scemo."*

Percy could see a dock washed by the waves. And what was that? A small motorboat bobbed about, smashing into the wooden dock over and over.

"What a fool the owner of that boat is," said Graziella. "It will be destroyed in this storm."

Her words sank in slowly. There was a boat. And it was doomed. So it was as though it belonged to no one. A surge of energy filled Percy. Before he even knew what he would do, he ran out of the restaurant, letting the door shut on the shouts from inside. He ran through the driving rain, ran and ran, all the way across the cemetery to the water. The sea was savage.

Graziella appeared beside him.

"I'm going back to Venice," he shouted above the scream of the wind. "I have to find Christopher. And Matteo." He ran out onto the dock.

Graziella ran beside him. "You cannot take the boat."

"I can't think about theft now, Graziella. Anyway, you said the boat would get destroyed in the storm."

"That is not what I mean. You cannot go across the water now. You will sink. You will die."

Percy looked at the sea. It wasn't that bad yet, really. He had to keep perspective. He wouldn't sail in a sea like this, but a motorboat was another thing. "I'll be fine."

"Listen, please." Graziella hung on his arm. "Please. Even the *vaporetto* does not go now. You know this. Please."

"The *vaporetto* is big and flat-bottomed. It would turn over easy. This little boat can maneuver through the waves. I'll make it." Percy moved to the edge and prepared to jump into the boat.

Graziella held his arm tighter. "I will not let you. No Venetian man would get in the boat now."

"Back home I sail boats all the time, Graziella. And I'm

a lifeguard. That means I can swim great. And it means I've promised to save lives from drowning. And it's my brother. My only brother. My little brother." Percy wrenched his arm free and jumped. The boat flew up on a wave at that very moment. Percy's right leg smashed into the side of the boat, but he tumbled forward and landed inside. He rubbed his shin and got to his knees. "Untie the rope and throw it to me," he shouted.

"I come, too." Graziella struggled with the rope knot.

"You said yourself: No Venetian would get in now."

"No Venetian man."

"No! I can't be responsible for you."

"That is right." Graziella finally managed to get the rope free. She held it tight and leaped. She slammed into Percy's chest.

"You're crazy. Can you even swim?"

But Graziella was already at the motor. "I know this kind." She pushed a button that Percy realized must be a primer—like on his lawn mower. Then she pulled the cord and the motor started.

The sea grew ever more angry. The sky was a swirl of dark gray. The wind whipped at their clothes and stung their eyes. Water splashed on them so relentlessly that sometimes Percy had to gasp for air. He could hardly see where they were going. But Graziella pointed expertly, and he steered where she pointed with blind trust. His heart pumped hard; he felt it would explode. He could do this. He had to.

Percy held the rudder handle so tight, his hand went white and numb. The boat bounced harder than ever and both of them flew up into the air and crash-landed. Percy scrambled back to the rudder handle and Graziella kneeled in the middle of the bottom of the boat and pointed. If the boat were to bounce even harder, if Graziella were to fly over the side, Percy knew he'd never find her in those waves. The words of that cursed sign came back to him: MEN DON'T PROTECT YOU ANYMORE. Percy certainly couldn't protect Graziella if she flew over the side. And if he were to fly over the side, he knew he'd never work his way back to the boat. What had he been thinking?

He hadn't been thinking. He'd just gotten into the boat.

This was insane.

Suicide.

Death at sea.

Death in Venice.

No! Percy held the rudder handle with both hands and fought the waves. He stared into the rain, desperate for a sign of land.

It seemed they were on the water for hours. The noise of the wind deafened him. His eyes ran, his nose ran, his head spun.

Still, Graziella pointed. Percy knew she couldn't see

through the pounding rain any better than he could. He knew she had to be guessing. But she didn't waver. She shouted directions firmly. And he followed them just as firmly. They were a team. Whether they drowned or lived, they were a team right now. He clenched his teeth and thought on that fact: Graziella and Percy were a team. And they wouldn't fail. They couldn't.

Lightning flashed close behind and an instant later the thunder boomed. Percy turned his face to the lightning and thought he saw a building back there. How? Where could they be that a building would be behind them now?

The boat bounced harder. Graziella flew upward. Percy stood and grabbed her to him. They both fell backward into the center of the boat. If he hadn't caught her, she'd have gone over that time. The knowledge threatened to make him weak kneed. But he couldn't afford that. He held one arm around her waist now and steered the rudder with the other hand. Such a small boat, getting smaller all the time. Such a large sea.

Crash!

The boat had smashed against something big. They would die now. This was it.

But, oh, it was a *fondamenta*. And the water had already risen a lot. It splashed over the edge. Graziella jumped out. *"Subito! Vieni!"*

Percy jumped out behind her, letting the boat spin away on the waves.

They ran through a huge open space. Puddles formed before their eyes. Percy realized they were in the Piazza San Marco. And now they sloshed through alleys, through tunnels, faster and faster, with Graziella leading.

"Wait!" Percy pulled her to him. "If I were caught in the storm and afraid of high water, I'd head for the highest point I knew." He nodded for emphasis. "Christopher is at the Scalzi Bridge."

"The Rialto is the highest," said Graziella.

"I know. But Christopher doesn't know. If he's not inside, if he didn't manage to find shelter, he's on the Scalzi." Percy could have kicked himself for forgetting to correct Christopher. The Rialto was much closer to San Marco than the Scalzi. If Percy had told Christopher, Christopher would have been at the Rialto now and Percy would have had him in his arms within minutes.

"Okay. The Scalzi. This way." Graziella turned and led Percy through more alleys, across small bridges, turning and turning.

They passed no one, literally no one. Not even a gull.

Finally they came out at the Scalzi Bridge. It was washed clean and shone white through the sheet of rain. And it was empty.

Percy's heart fell.

"*Tocca a me,*" said Graziella. "It is my turn. I believe they are in church."

Percy looked dumbfounded. "Christopher would hardly even recognize a church."

"Matteo will feel safe in church. Church is home to people like him—the ones who are not ordinary. He has taken Christopher to church, I am positive."

Percy shook his head. "Christopher told me everyone says Matteo has no brains. He wouldn't put his trust in Matteo like that."

"Of course he would. Christopher is not *stupido*. He knows Matteo has been through floods—he knows Matteo understands some things. *Vieni*." Graziella ran, over the bridge, along the Lista di Spagna, straight for Don Bosco.

Percy swallowed his doubt and followed her. The path was an inch under water or more. The buildings on both sides were shuttered all the way up. No one looked out. No one would see two lost little boys.

Percy ran faster, splashing through the water. He passed Graziella and raced for the church.

The huge wood doors had been drawn shut. Together Graziella and Percy pulled one open enough to enter. Percy was amazed that it hadn't been bolted. But, then, churches were supposed to offer haven, weren't they? Maybe it was immoral to bolt them. But, oh, Christopher and Matteo could never have opened that heavy door by themselves. So this church was as good as bolted for them.

The door banged shut behind them, leaving the roar of

the wind outside. They heard it now only as though from a great distance. The church was hushed and empty.

Percy looked around. No one in the pews. No one in the aisles. He fought tears. "Christopher, where are you?"

"Percy?" said Christopher's high voice.

Percy swung around.

Christopher came out from under the altar wearing his backpack over his raincoat—that beloved backpack. Matteo came out, too. Christopher ran to Percy. Matteo ran to Graziella.

Christopher jumped into Percy's arms, wrapping his legs around his waist and hugging him tight. "Oh, Percy, you didn't drown."

"Neither did you, Christopher. Oh, neither did you." Percy buried his face in Christopher's neck and breathed in the smells of milk and jam and bread and peach. The essence of little brother. And the tears Percy had held back fell hot on Christopher's cheek.

CHAPTER 19

Percy wound Graziella's braid around his wrist. She leaned back against him and they looked out over the water that passed under the Scalzi Bridge. The storm was two days in the past now, but the canals were still full of debris. He tugged gently on her braid. Her hair seemed to glow in the sunlight.

Graziella turned slightly and nestled under Percy's arm. "A miracle," she said slowly, "can be a terrible thing."

A miracle. Percy hadn't thought about the flood being a miracle. But that was what it was to Graziella and Alessandro and Claudio and all the other politicos at the club. The storm had done exactly what they'd hoped: The commission in charge had turned down Venice's offer the day after the storm. Expo would take place somewhere else. The club had held a celebration party the night before.

Percy never found out whether Alessandro and Claudio had pulled the lever on the transformer for the floodgate. Whether they had or not, the floodgate wouldn't have gone up—so he didn't ask. And, in truth, he didn't want to know.

And Dad had taken the failure of MOSE pretty well. After all, it wasn't MOSE itself that failed; the electricity for all Venice had gone out, and then the backup generator had died. Percy hadn't even known there was a backup generator. According to Dad, the CNR should have arranged it so that each of the three independent generators at the three floodgates served as backup for the two others. He had suggested that arrangement right from the start. But everyone thought the likelihood of both Venice's electricity going out and a generator dying was remote. So the generators at each port were entirely separate units. It was just rotten luck that lightning had struck the one at San Pietro in Volta—the one that backed up the floodgate at the Porto di Malamocco. Whatever, the MOSE project continued undaunted. And Dad's enthusiasm was as strong as ever.

All the loose strands that had made Percy feel the world was coming apart just a few days ago were now back together. Maybe they weren't woven into a rope yet, but at least they adhered to one another.

"Come on." Percy let go of Graziella's braid and took her by the hand. "Let's have a coffee and decide how to spend the afternoon."

They walked along the *fondamenta*. Graziella made a purring noise.

"You're like a kitten."

"A kitten? Me?" Graziella growled.

Percy laughed. "A lion cub, then."

Graziella smiled. "That is better. Okay, we go decide how to pass our vacation."

They'd been working nonstop along with everyone else at Estate Ragazzi to clean up the mess from the storm. They had swept piles of garbage to the edges of *campos*— cardboard boxes, crates, fruits, broken glass, ripped awnings. They'd washed store floors and windows. They'd repaired doors and furniture. But at the end of work this morning the priests had told them all to take off the afternoon and help with their own families' storm damage. Percy's parents didn't have any storm damage, of course. And Graziella's grandmother lived a quiet indoor life, so the storm hadn't touched her directly, either. That meant that Percy and Graziella were free for the afternoon.

"*Ho un'idea*. I have an idea." Graziella quickly changed direction and led Percy to the boat stop. They took the crowded *vaporetto* down the Canal Grande to Piazza San Marco.

The piazza was riddled with puddles, but already some spots were chalky dry in the sun. They walked quickly across the piazza and through the well-marked alleys. Graziella looked up at Percy with fun in her eyes. "Come, *Signor Leone,* Mr. Lion, this way."

They turned down one of the narrowest alleys Percy had been in yet, one that was still a couple of inches under water, and headed straight for a canal. Percy imagined Graziella leaping over the canal gracefully (true to her name) and him following and landing splat in the water. But at the end of the alley, no one leapt. Instead, they turned left under a portico and then right over a small iron bridge, and then right and left again and walked up a long, relatively wide alley.

"Look," said Graziella, pointing to the doors. *"Grrrrrr."*

There were lion heads on almost every door. Some were doorknobs. Others were door knockers. There were lion heads chiseled in stone around the cornices of the windows and others sticking out from under the edges of the roofs like gargoyles.

"I have to bring Christopher here," said Percy.

"Yes. He will like it."

They went back to the piazza, sat at a side bar, and ordered espresso. Percy watched Graziella put one teaspoon of sugar in her tiny cup. Then a second. Then a third. He was amazed. The woman had a massive sweet tooth. Was she going to take a fourth? Instead, she stirred the thick mud that had started out as decent coffee. She took a sip.

Percy smiled. "Tell me, why do you drink coffee if you hate it?"

"*Cosa?* I do not hate coffee."

"But you can't even taste it with all that sugar in there."

Graziella smiled. "You take it black?"

"You bet," said Percy. He took a sip. "This is marvelous."

"You are Turk," said Graziella.

"Is that an insult?"

"It is fact." She sipped again.

Percy looked around at all the bustle in the piazza. "It's amazing how normal things seem."

"People must eat. Markets must have food. And tourists must not have inconvenience."

Tourists. Percy felt the blood rush to his face. "It amazes me how we can be together, just you and me, and be so happy. And then . . ."

Graziella looked at him. "And then?"

"Then suddenly a whole wall of tourists separates us."

Graziella nodded. "You want to ignore the, how do you say, the real things. The realities."

"But we're real, Graziella." Percy took her hand. "You and me. Some real things are more important than others."

Graziella looked at him with troubled eyes.

"Your need to stop Expo was real, and your need to protect Matteo and Christopher was real."

Graziella nodded slowly. "Yes. One real thing can be more important than another. Yes. But how do you know which? In the storm it was clear. I knew. But how do you know in general? How can you be sure?"

"You decide," said Percy.

She squeezed his hand. "You have an optimistic soul."

"So do you," said Percy. "It takes optimism to fight the system."

"Optimism?" Graziella's eyes glittered as though she held back tears. "I always thought it was desperation."

A young woman walking by stopped suddenly. "Graziella!" She ran over and kissed Graziella on both cheeks. Graziella introduced her to Percy as Angela and then the two women talked rapidly and emotionally and Angela raced off, calling, *"Ci vediamo presto."*

"Who is she?" asked Percy.

"My good friend who lives on the Lido. The damage there is much worse than here. She said it is a shame that the Lido does not have the *Murazzi* that Pellestrina has."

"What are the *Murazzi*?"

"Oh, you have never seen them?" Graziella's eyes went wide. "You must." She leaned toward him and spoke with conviction. "Today."

Percy laughed. "What are they?"

"You need to see them to understand."

"You've got me." Percy brushed Graziella's braid back and cupped her shoulder with his hand. "Let's go."

The *vaporetto* to the Lido overflowed with people talking and laughing. Percy could see worry on some faces. But mostly people were happy that the storm hadn't been worse. The atmosphere was almost like that of a holiday. A man in the row of seats behind Percy and Graziella passed out plastic cups to the people with him and poured champagne. Percy wasn't sure, but he thought the man was saying something about a boat not turning over. The lagoon was dotted with boats, in fact. Not as many as usual, but still plenty. There were even a few sailboats.

Percy and Graziella got out at the Lido, walked down the avenue, and got to the bus stop just as the bus was arriving. They rode the full length of the island, holding hands, lost in thought.

The bus stopped at Alberoni and more than half the people on board got off. Then it rode right onto the ferry. The bus driver hit a button and the doors opened. He got off.

Graziella led Percy off the bus, too. They wove their way through the parked cars on the ferry and stood at the railing. The wind was gentle and warm. The sea was as calm and smooth as Graziella's lips. It glistened. The sun set the sky aflame in pinks and yellows.

Percy held both hands on the railing and leaned over the

side. Graziella stood behind him and stretched her arms out to either side, holding on to the railing just inside his hands. He could feel her cheek resting on his back. Gulls flew overhead and cried.

The bus horn sounded. The driver was already in his seat. People climbed back on board. Graziella and Percy got on but stayed standing in the aisle. The ferry landed and the bus motor roared. The bus rolled onto land and continued down the long island, all the way to Pellestrina.

Graziella and Percy got off and faced the tiny village. They crossed the road to the sea side of the island, away from the village. There was a wall of enormous rocks and blocks of stone along the shore. It stood taller than Percy. Graziella climbed up the wall and sat facing the water. Percy sat beside her.

"These are the *Murazzi*. These seawalls."

Percy put his palms flat on the warm stone.

"They were built in the seventeen hundreds, before Napoleone invaded Venice, to save the island, this island. The town across the road is called Pellestrina. But the whole island, really it is not an island, it is a, how do you say, sandbar, the whole sandbar is also called Pellestrina. The people built this wall to keep Pellestrina from being washed away in storms."

Percy rubbed the rough white-and-gray rock. "They're huge."

"Yes. These are giant blocks of stone from Istria. Do you know Istria?"

Percy shook his head. "Is it in Italy?"

"Istria is a peninsula that belonged to Italy but now is part of Slovenia." Graziella pointed to the south. "The *Murazzi* were built first at that end, the southern end, of Pellestrina, at the Porto di Chioggia. But later they extended them all along the island." She turned to Percy and smiled. "They have kept the island from washing away. They have done their job well."

"It's a magnificent wall," said Percy. He stood up. The wall was maybe four feet wide there. "Want to walk along it?"

"*Sì.*"

They walked northward, the sun getting lower on their right. The wet sand at the sea side of the wall was littered with white moving things. "What are those?"

"Ghost crabs. They come out as the tide gets low."

Percy stopped suddenly and turned. He caught Graziella as she took a step after him. He held her by the upper arms. "I've been thinking about what we were talking about before—about optimism and desperation."

Graziella looked into his face. "And what is your thought, *Stracciatella*?"

"A person driven by optimism will do risky things."

"A person driven by desperation will do risky things," said Graziella.

Percy nodded. "A person driven by optimism will push for change."

"A person driven by desperation will push for change," said Graziella.

Percy nodded. "A person driven by optimism will keep the best of the past even into the future."

"A person driven by desperation will keep . . ." She screwed up her mouth. ". . . will do the same. All the things you said."

Percy nodded. "So they look the same sometimes. You can get confused." He ran his hands down her arms and took her hands. He pulled them to his chest. "But there's a difference."

"Dimmi," said Graziella.

"A person driven by optimism thinks anything can happen. That person can fall in love, even when things seem hard. And—I think I'm in love with you."

Graziella's lips parted slightly as she looked solemnly at Percy. "And I think I am in love with you, also." She kissed him softly. "And I thank you."

Percy cocked his head. "You thank me?"

"You helped me put the love of Matteo and Christopher first. You taught me optimism."

Percy caressed Graziella's cheek. "I've been thinking about other things, too."

Graziella smiled. *"Stracciatella,* the chocolate-chip thinker."

"I care about how things work. It's hard to grow up with an engineer for a father and not get that way."

Graziella nodded.

"I'm going with my dad to the CNR every other day from now on. That way I can spend one day at the Estate Ragazzi and one day with him."

Graziella bit her bottom lip. "But . . . why?"

"I'm here for the summer. I might as well take each day at a time. I've thought it through . . ."

She nodded. "Yes, big, bold thinker."

Bold. She was right: Percy felt bold. "I can't be a Venetian, Graziella. We both know that. But we can't let thoughts of the future ruin the present. We are here, both of us, together now in Venice. That's how it is."

Graziella's eyes were luminous. "I am very glad that you have come to Venice," she whispered.

"So am I. Maybe I can find something interesting to work on at the CNR. A project I can help with. Maybe I can convince them I'm useful enough that they'll want me to come back to Venice next summer. And this winter— I'll study Italian! Study *hard*."

"Thoughts of the future," said Graziella softly.

Percy grinned. "And you know what else?"

"There is more?" said Graziella.

"Yes." Percy reached into his pocket and pulled out a 100,000-lire bill. "Dad gave me an advance, as payment for something I'm going to do for him. Would you like a real dinner? I mean, not just pizza."

"An expensive dinner? Do you think I could agree to such a *borghese*—bourgeois—experience? Anyway, I love pizza, *Stracciatella*."

"So do I," said Percy. "But sometimes a celebration is in order."

"A celebration," said Graziella.

"There are things that must be celebrated."

"*O, sì.*" Graziella smiled. "You are right. Again. And afterward I will take you to my *gelateria*."

"And I will order *stracciatella*," said Percy. "And what flavor will you give me?"

"Wait, my new wonderful engineer. Wait and see."